VICE, REDEMPTION
AND THE
DISTANT COLONY

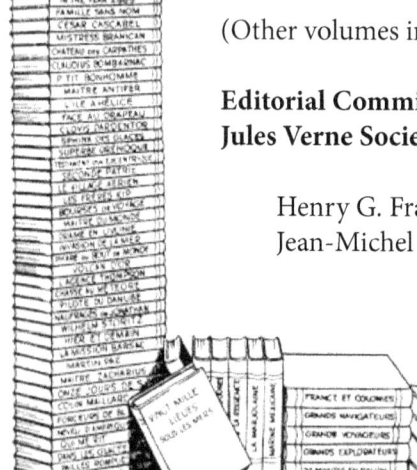

Vice, Redemption and the Distant Colony

And the

Distant Colony

Stories by Jules Verne
and Michel Verne

Translated, with notes, by Kieran M. O'Driscoll

Edited by Brian Taves
for the North American Jules Verne Society

The Palik Series

BearManor Fiction

2012

Vice, Redemption and the Distant Colony
by Jules Verne and Michel Verne

For information, address:

BearManor Fiction
P. O. Box 71426
Albany, GA 31708

bearmanormedia.com

North American Jules Verne Society: najvs.org

Typesetting and layout by John Teehan

Cover design from an original 19th century French edition

Back cover illustration from *Aventures de trois Russes et de trois Anglais dans l'Afrique australe* (*Adventures of Three Russians and Three Englishmen in Southern Africa*, 1872)

Published in the USA by BearManor Media

ISBN—1-59393-377-0
978-1-59393-377-7

Table of Contents

For Neil, John, Alice and Aiden,
and also dedicated lovingly to the memory of
Nora, Frank and Lal O'Driscoll,
much-loved mother, father
and grandmother.

Jules Verne in 1902, three years before his death.

Introduction

A Familial Collaboration

In this volume of the North American Jules Verne Society's Palik series, we celebrate a collaboration unique in literary history. This joining of father and son began while both were alive, and was continued after the father's death in the creative efforts of the son, both in prose and on the movie screen. That the father is the celebrated French author Jules Verne makes the importance of the joint creative efforts of these two individuals all the more important.

In 1856 Jules Verne met Honorine du Fraysne de Viane, a twenty-six year old widow with two young daughters. Jules and Honorine married on 10th January, 1857. He sought financial assistance from both his father and his father-in-law in order to establish himself as a stockbroker. The couple's only child, Michel Jean Pierre Verne, was born in 1861.

Jules Gabriel Verne's own birth had been in 1828 in Nantes. His childhood was spent in the maritime bustle of this trading port, as ships arrived and departed on long voyages. These tropes of travel were so much in evidence as to inculcate a love for travel and adventure, suggesting the themes of journeys and discovery in his fiction.

Verne's father Pierre was a solicitor. His mother, Sophie Allotte de la Fuye, came from a well-to-do Nantes family which included ship owners and navigators. Together, the family claimed French, Breton and Scottish ancestry.

Unlike his own son, who only had the companionship of his stepsisters, Jules had a younger brother, Paul, born in 1829. The two brothers were to remain very close throughout their whole lives. The

1

The Verne family, seated, father, mother, and son, at Mers-les-Bains, France, 1894.

Verne family was later further extended with the birth of three sisters, Anna, Mathilde and Marie.

In 1844, Jules was enrolled as a pupil at the *Lycée royal* of Nantes, graduating with his *baccalauréat* in 1846. As his father's intention was that Jules would follow in his footsteps as a member of the legal profession, thus eventually assuming control of the family legal practice, Jules began, in 1847, to study law. He had also begun to indulge in creative writing, initially for his own recreation and pleasure.

As Verne was becoming increasingly resolved to establish a reputation as a playwright, he convinced his father to allow him to move to Paris, a city of numerous theatres, in 1848. He continued his legal studies there, obtaining his law degree in 1848. In 1850, he became acquainted with Alexandre Dumas *père* and *fils*. With their assistance, Verne's play *Les Pailles Rompues* (*Broken Straws*, 1850) was staged at the *Théâtre-Historique*, to popular acclaim.

Though 1850 was the year in which Verne defended his law thesis, he refused to assume control of his father's legal practice, as he had made up his mind to pursue a literary career. However, in order to earn a living while he sought to establish himself as a writer and dramatist, he did give some private law lessons and did some part-time legal work.

In 1852, he became secretary to Jules Seveste, manager of the *Théâtre-Lyrique*, and continued to write for the stage (several plays written by Jules Verne are included in a previous volume in the Palik series, *Mr. Chimp, and Other Plays*). He began to publish short stories and serialised novels in a magazine entitled *Musée des Familles* (*Family Museum*), including such stories as "Un voyage en Ballon" ("A Balloon Journey," 1851) and *Martin Paz* (1852). Hence, Verne only gradually emerged as a creative writer, after dabbling in a series of different professions. Not until 1862 did Verne's literary career begin to become very successful, with the publication of his novel *Cinq Semaines en Ballon* (*Five Weeks in a Balloon*), which enjoyed great success worldwide.

His celebrated novel *Voyage au Centre de la Terre* (*Voyage to the Center of the Earth*) was published in 1864, with *De la Terre à la Lune* (*From the Earth to the Moon*) being published the following year. Verne began to publish regularly in a newly-created magazine aimed at younger readers, founded by his publisher, Pierre-Jules Hetzel, entitled *Magasin d'Education et de Récréation*. Verne discontinued his employment at the Stock Exchange in order to devote himself to writing full-time.

From the publication of these earliest novels onwards, Jules Verne attracted what some commentators have labelled a "dual" readership. This consisted, first, of younger readers who thrilled to the adventurous dimension of Verne's œuvre, and, second, older readers who enjoyed the aspects of scientific pedagogy, discovery and exploration in his novels, but who did not fail to equally appreciate the imaginative and fantastic aspects, and the dramatic storytelling style, of the theatrical writer which Verne the novelist essentially remained. The stated goal of what became the "Voyages Extraordinaires" ("Extraordinary Journeys") series was explained by Hetzel, who stated: "Son but est de résumer toutes les connaissances géographiques, géologiques, physiques, astonomiques, amassées par la science moderne, et de refaire, sous la forme attrayante et pittoresque qui lui est propre, l'histoire de l'univers." ("Its mission is to summarize all of the geographical, geological, physical and astronomical knowledge built up by modern science and to rewrite, in its characteristically attractive and picturesque format, the history of the universe.")

In 1866, Verne purchased a fishing boat which he named the *Saint-Michel*, after his son, and this marked the beginning of his enduring passion for sea journeys. A year later Verne crossed the Atlantic aboard the *Great Eastern*, a vessel which laid a transatlantic telephone cable between France and the United States. Upon his return to France, Verne began to write what many consider to be his masterpiece, *Vingt Mille Lieues sous les Mers* (*Twenty Thousand Leagues Under the Seas*, 1869). Captain Nemo, the complex, mysterious and solitary central character, is felt to be one of Verne's most fascinating fictional creations. Much of this novel was written aboard the *Saint-Michel*, which Verne dubbed his "floating study."

Verne worked as a coastguard in 1870 during the Franco-Prussian war. His brother Paul, a member of the Navy, had fought in the Crimean War in 1854.

Verne's father Pierre died in 1871, and the following year Jules Verne and his family moved to Amiens, his wife's birthplace. Verne was at the peak of his literary success as a writer of popular literature, sustaining an incredibly prodigious rate of literary output and of publications. One of his most celebrated novels, *Le Tour du Monde en Quatre-Vingts Jours* (*Around the World in Eighty Days*), was published in 1873, and he co-authored a hugely popular theatrical adaptation of this landmark novel the following year (this play is also to be included in the Palik series). Verne purchased a yacht which he christened the *Saint-Michel II*, and his novel *L'Île Mystérieuse* (*The Mysterious Island*) was completed in 1875, closing the saga of Captain Nemo.

The string of successes continued with the publication of *Michel Strogoff* in 1876. However, unlike the eponymous hero of this Jules Verne novel, Michel Verne had behaved in a wanton, irresponsible manner that went beyond the accepted boundariess of the time. He was sent by his father to Mettray Penal Colony in 1876, for six months, aged fifteen.

Michel had far exceeded the relatively mild rebelliousness of his father's youth, in which Jules had manifested his determination not to assume control of his father's legal practice, but to instead pursue a writing career. There had also been other instances of rebellion on Jules' part, but only when he was a boy. A notable and often recounted episode from his childhood is that, in 1839, at the age of eleven, he ran away from home, embarking as a ship's boy on a long-haul voyage bound for the Indies. His later confessed objective was to bring back a coral necklace for his cousin Caroline, for whom he bore an unrequited love. His father caught up with him at Paimboeuf, France, and the young Jules promised that, in future, his only travels would be "en rêve" ("in dreams").

As Jules purchased yet another yacht, the *Saint-Michel III*, he undertook several prolonged sea journeys, visiting such regions as the Mediterranean, Scotland and the Baltic Sea. Michel was recruited as a ship's boy on a vessel bound for the Indies. Returning to Europe, Michel accumulated heavy debts over a number of years, and also suffered alcohol-abuse problems.

When he was nineteen, Michel created a scandal by eloping with an actress, disregarding the objections of his father. Though Michel married her in 1883, he abandoned her shortly afterward and ran away with sixteen-year-old Jeanne Reboul, who bore him two children prior to his divorce being finalized.

Jules's own romances had met with frequent failure. He suffered romantic heartbreak, owing to the marriage of his cousin Caroline, with whom he had been smitten for many years. In the mid 1850s, Verne's parents tried unsuccessfully to arrange a suitable marriage for him, to, successively, various young ladies from comfortably-off Nantes families. His marriage to Honorine was troubled, and he was believed to have a mistress, although this could never be confirmed, Jules having always been notoriously discreet about his private life.

A turning point for the worse in the life of Jules Verne came in 1886. That year, he was wounded by two bullets fired in a gunshot attack by his mentally disturbed nephew Gaston, an attack thought to be provoked, at least in part, by Verne's refusal to lend him money. Verne was badly affected, physically and psychologically, by this attack, in the aftermath of which he never fully regained the degree of mobility he had previously enjoyed. His lifelong publisher, Hetzel, also died that year, with his son taking over the firm.

Verne's mother passed away in 1887. Giving up his travels, Verne decided to devote himself to local politics. The following year, he was elected as a local representative on the municipal council of Amiens.

These events began the process of reconciling Jules and Michel. By 1889, Michel was beginning to write his own short stories, with his father's encouragement. Two of these were published in English, "In

Michel at age 7, and age 30, by which time he begun collaborating with his father.

the Year 2889" and "An Express of the Future," under the Jules Verne byline. Jules did not mind, and created his own version of his son's story of the millennium hence. While Michel pursued business and other ventures, they collaborated on some writings, and Michel continued to pen stories of his own. At least one of his novels, *L'Agence Thompson and Co.* (*The Agency Thompson and Co.*), Jules intended to include in the "Extraordinary Journeys," and it appeared that way posthumously in 1907, under the father's byline.

In 1897, Verne's brother Paul died. The writer's own health also began to significantly deteriorate around this time. Nevertheless, he continued to write and publish right up to his final illness, so that he can be seen to have remained consistently prolific in his literary output throughout his long and glowing publishing career. He died on 24th March, 1905, aged seventy-seven.

Michel took charge of publishing many of his father's final manuscripts posthumously. There were, for a long time, unsubstantiated rumours that Michel may have written some of them himself; recent evidence, in the form of the original manuscripts, reveals that this was indeed the case. Some of Michel's efforts involved changes to the early and/or unfinished texts written by Jules, while in other cases, he created new, original literary texts. Nonetheless, the Jules Verne name appeared on all the stories, even when partly or entirely the writing of Michel Verne.

This was not the first such influence on the writings of Jules Verne. Verne and his publisher, Pierre-Jules Hetzel, had a lifelong collaboration, and the publisher had a significant influence on Verne's writings, often suggesting and imposing alterations to the style and the plots of different novels. Some literary commentators see this particular collaboration between publisher and author as a positive, joint creative process. Others see Hetzel's sometimes active involvement in the revision of the novels as negative and interfering, with Hetzel diluting their literary merit in order to maximize their potential commercial success. Now, with the author's death, Michel had to contend with the editing of Hetzel *fils*.

The present volume explores the literary partnership between Jules and Michel in different ways. The third story which features in the present volume, *Fact-Finding Mission* (original French title: *Voyages d'Etudes*, literally, *Study Trip*) was an unfinished novel by Jules, which Michel extended into a long, complete novel, attributed to his father, called *L'Etonnante Aventure de la Mission Barsac* (literally, this title translates as *The Astonishing Adventure of the Barsac Mission*). This novel has been translated into English in 1960 by I.O. Evans in two parts, respectively entitled *Into the Niger Bend* and *The City in the Sahara*, and fortunately thanks to paperback publication, those books remain inexpensively available on the second-hand market. However, the original text of the novel begun by Jules Verne has never appeared in English before, only Michel's rewrite.

The Barsac Mission was serialized in 1914; by that time Michel had begun a company to produce his father's stories for the screen. With the emergence of longer films of an hour or more, Michel used the newest performance medium of the 20th century to present his father's stories, just as Jules had adapted his novels into stage spectaculars of the 19th century.

Among the volumes that represented the joint efforts of father and son was *Hier et demain*. This book of short stories followed an outline of Jules for an anthology, which had remained unpublished by

COLLECTION HETZEL

— HIER ET DEMAIN —

CONTES & NOUVELLES

The frontispiece of *Yesterday and Tomorrow* (1910).

Hetzel. However, Michel changed much of the planned contents. One of the stories he decided to include was his father's *Pierre-Jean,* which Michel reworked into an extended and dramatically altered version entitled *La Destinée de Jean Morénas.* In turn, Michel went on to adapt it for the cinema in 1915. In this volume, both literary versions of this story, that of the father and that of the son, are translated together for the first time into English.

Michel Verne, as an individual author and film-maker, in his own right, has only comparatively recently begun to emerge from the long shadow cast by his famous father. His role in the creation of some of the later *Extraordinary Journeys* remained unknown at the time of his death in 1925. This volume, in offering stories by both Jules and Michel, under the by-line of both, honors father and son, and seeks to reveal more clearly the true, full extent of a "collaboration" that has only become apparent in recent times. The North American Jules Verne Society salutes the imaginative skill and creative ability of both men.

Foreword

Pierre-Jean and *The Sombre Fate of Jean Morénas*

"**I**t doesn't matter where you've been as long as you come back strong." The tagline of Gwyneth Paltrow's new movie *Country Strong* seems also an appropriate slogan for two of the stories translated here: Jules Verne's novella *Pierre-Jean,* and his son Michel's later reworking of this story into a longer novella entitled *La Destinée de Jean Morénas*, which I have translated here as *The Sombre Fate of Jean Morénas* (hereinafter referred to as *Morénas*). In both of these lesser-known Verne novellas, as in the above-mentioned Paltrow movie, a courageous and resilient protagonist shows admirable determination in struggling to start a new life, following a prolonged period of suffering and oppression. But will stoutness of heart lead to a happy ending for the risk-taker? Readers who are not yet familiar with these two newly-translated, lesser-known Verne novellas or the film, are advised not to read this Foreword until they have first enjoyed the stories themselves; this comparison of the two versions of a Verne adventure story—and of their subsequent film version—inevitably contains "spoilers."

Both Verne stories deal with a central character who has been sentenced to a fixed-term period of penal servitude in the former port-based penal colony at Toulon. The sentence has been increased in severity, as punishment for a failed escape bid, in the case of the *Morénas* story, and as a consequence of re-offending following initial release, in the case of *Pierre-Jean.* The convict in question, who is the central character in each of the two versions, has now been manacled in double chains to a fellow prisoner, and is working as a "galley slave," at the outset of both stories.

11

In both versions, which appear to be set in the early nineteenth century, a mysterious stranger—a wealthy, reserved and discreet businessman called Monsieur Bernardon, based in Marseilles—one day seeks authorization to visit the penal colony, on the pretext of acquainting himself, for philanthropic purposes, with the various prison workshops and the lives and conditions of the prisoners. However, it turns out that his benevolent intentions are specifically directed, not at the entire prison community, but rather at one particular convict, prisoner number 2,224. This convict is known, in the original story by Verne *père*, as Pierre-Jean; and, in the version by Verne *fils*, as Jean Morénas. The protagonist is an honest and intelligent young man, who yearns for freedom, but has resigned himself to enduring his degrading, backbreaking existence as a convict. In the version as rewritten by Michel Verne, using the inspiration of his father's original narrative, the hero, Jean Morénas, is innocent of the murder for which he has been imprisoned, and discovers towards the end of the story that the actual killer—of his uncle, Alexandre Tisserand ("Uncle Sandy")—is his long-lost older brother, Pierre, who also turns out to be "M. Bernardon," his disguised mysterious benefactor who twice visits him on the docks of the port-based prison. But in Jules Verne's original, the hero, Pierre-Jean Renaud, is guilty of the various thefts for which he has been imprisoned; yet in spite of past failings, he, too, is a basically virtuous and courageous person.

Offered the means of escape, and the chance to start a new life, by the mysterious visitor, the central character in each story seizes the opportunity presented to him, and swims with all the strength he can muster to a designated spot at which he is reunited with his enigmatic saviour. While swimming through the port of the naval prison, and later through the open sea, the hero comes close to being recaptured, but succeeds in skilfully outwitting his pursuers, resolving to himself that he will sooner drown than return to the hell of the penal colony. Indeed, he does come close to drowning, because of his rapidly diminishing strength, at several stages during his heroic swim for freedom, but nevertheless reaches shore, where he collapses with exhaustion. He is there revived through the brandy given to him by "M. Bernardon."

At this point, Michel Verne's retelling of the story diverges substantially from that of his father. In the Jules Verne original, the

Victor Hugo, a literary idol of Jules Verne.

hero makes a further exhausting journey, alone, through the fields, woods and mountains of the Toulon countryside, wearing a disguise given him by his benefactor. At one point, he is apparently recaptured by three men, but these turn out to be allies of M. Bernardon, who are, in reality, making sure that the escapee does not fall back into the hands of the pursuing *brigades de gendarmerie* (squads of police officers). These men bring him to a small, humble abode on the outskirts of the village of Sainte-Marie-des-Maures, where Pierre-Jean is once again brought face-to-face with his "savior" whose real name, in this original version, is indeed Bernardon, and who is not the protagonist's brother, as in Michel's version.

It is at this point that the dénouement to the mystery is presented. Pierre-Jean, as we are now informed by Bernardon in his explanation to the escapee, had been released from prison three years previously, following five years of penal servitude for crimes of theft which had been, in sum, out of character for this essentially good human being: "There had certainly never been any evil intentions in his heart; in a moment of error, he had fallen by the wayside, but his severe punishment, far from corrupting him by placing him in the company of all sorts of villains, had spurred him on to good and serious reflections; he wished to see his elderly mother again, to support her... and to love her with all his heart." (Chapter 5)

But upon his release, he had encountered an old woman who was about to be evicted from her cottage unless she could come up with fifty francs in rent; taking pity on her, Pierre-Jean had given her this sum, which was all the money he then possessed. This old woman, who is now also present as this story is recounted, was, it turns out, the mother of his grateful rescuer. Pierre-Jean, in a further moment of desperation, had gone on to steal back the fifty francs from the bailiff who had collected them from the old woman; this moment of weakness and temptation meant that he was sent back to prison.

It is because of the kindness he showed to M. Bernardon's mother, that Bernardon has now done everything in his power to help Pierre-Jean to escape from prison, and now gives him the opportunity to sail away from Marseilles that very evening "to the New World," to start a new life, with money in his pocket "which will forever keep you sheltered from financial need." (Chapter 5) Pierre-Jean promises his benefactor that he will work hard "if... for no other reason than to redeem myself in your eyes!" (Chapter 5) The story ends with the central character sailing towards the Strait of Gibraltar on the first leg of his voyage towards a new life.

Crime, punishment, mercy and redemption are thus themes of the original version of this story, by Jules Verne. But if these are also the central themes of Michel Verne's renarration, the happy ending provided by Jules Verne—a feature of so many of his works, often imposed by his publisher Hetzel in order to boost sales—becomes, in

Michel's version, a bitter end for the doomed, tragic protagonist Jean Morénas.[1]

Though the early chapters of Michel's version are, essentially, a sometimes word-for-word reiteration of the corresponding chapters of his father's original—as regards the detailed description of conditions at the penal colony, the encounters between the rescued convict and his rescuer, and the dramatic, superhuman endurance of the swim to freedom—the chapters of Michel's *Morénas* which deal with what happens after the hero makes good his escape differ significantly from those of Jules's *Pierre-Jean*. Michel's version is longer, darker, more complex and more tragic—yet ultimately more satisfying as an involved, gripping, suspenseful adventure story and crime mystery. It also has overtones of Shakespearian, Dostoyevskyian and Hugoesque tragedy: the reader is often reminded of the harsh prison regime suffered by the convict Valjean in Victor Hugo's *Les Misérables*. This famous 1862 French novel has usually been translated into English retaining the French title, which can be translated as "the poor; the wretched; the downtrodden," and so on, so I will hereafter refer to it simply as *Les Misérables*. There are parallels between the circumstances of Jean Morénas/Pierre-Jean, and Valjean's quest, in Hugo's novel, for a new life and for redemption, and his mercy towards others, all the while being relentlessly pursued by the repressive legal system, as personified by Inspector Javert.[2]

Jean Morénas—in Michel's version—having recovered his strength following his exhausting swim to safety, is accompanied through the Toulon countryside by his rescuer M. Bernardon, who also helps him to escape the pursuing *gendarmes* before leaving him alone, with money to start a new life, and passage on a ship bound for Valparaiso in Chile. It is only when his mysterious savior has vanished into the darkness as abruptly as he first appeared, that Jean realizes he does not even know the stranger's name, nor the reasons for his extraordinary kindness to him. He also quickly decides that he does not want to travel abroad to a new life—he wants to return to his native village and try to protest his innocence to his unrequited love, Marguerite (she is originally referred

---

1. The nature of the collaboration between Jules Verne and his publisher, Hetzel, is discussed by William Butcher in *Jules Verne: The Definitive Biography* (New York: Thunder's Mouth Press, 2006).

2. Hugo, Victor. *Les Misérables* (New York: New American Library, 1987).

to as Marie, but her name is inexplicably changed in the course of the story, most likely through a lapse on Michel Verne's part). Jean is also full of optimism that she may now, finally, reciprocate his love for her and agree to go away with him.

However, on his return to the inn formerly owned by his murdered uncle, Jean witnesses the attempted murder of the local solicitor, in the main room of the inn, by an assailant who turns out to be none other than his brother Pierre, whom he has not seen in fifteen years; and Pierre, stripped of his disguises such as a wig and false beard, turns out to be one and the same person as "M. Bernardon," his rescuer. Jean, watching, in terror and disbelief, from a hiding place within the large fireplace, his brother's strangulation of the local notary, and robbery of his banknotes, is at first more baffled than ever. He then deduces, largely correctly, the truth (which has already been apprehended by the reader, through the flashbacks and hints provided by the omniscient, third-person narrator): it was Pierre who murdered their Uncle Sandy and stole his money all those years ago. Jean had then been unjustly imprisoned for the crime, and Pierre had later returned to the village. He had won the heart of Marie/Marguerite, married her, had three children with her, and had become the wealthiest man in the village.

Jean feels that Pierre has ruined his life, and has taken from him everything that could have been his, especially the love of Marguerite. He is about to denounce Pierre, but then has second thoughts. Again showing his self-sacrificing qualities, he decides that he does not want to condemn Marguerite to a life of despair by having Pierre imprisoned. Nor does he want to shatter her illusions about the husband she clearly loves. He thus makes the ultimate gesture of heroic abnegation; he "confesses" to having attempted to rob and kill the local notary; does not protest his innocence of murdering his uncle, and abandons himself to his captors. He is even denied what he sees as the mercy of a death sentence for murder, as the notary has by now recovered consciousness.

As he leaves with his captors, he also realizes that his beloved Marguerite now hates him for the crimes he has "admitted" to. Conjuring up a consoling mental vision of Marguerite holding her youngest child in her arms, the tragic hero Jean walks calmly to his sombre destiny, "disappearing into the darkness." (Chapter 9)

The Film Version of *Morénas*

In the 1916 silent film version of *Morénas*—a film also made by Michel Verne—those who have already read the novella encounter a major twist at the end of the movie, which has hitherto remained very faithful to the literary text. There is a pleasant surprise in seeing that the movie uses a key plot change in order to provide a happy ending for Jean Morénas, as opposed to his tragic fate in the novella. In the cinematic adaptation, Marguerite witnesses the strangling of the notary, and thus knows that her husband Pierre is the culprit. Despite Jean's attempted "confession," it is Marguerite who informs the people present that Jean is not the killer. At this point, Pierre confesses to both murders (though the notary recovers consciousness in the novella, he dies in the film adaptation). Pierre then shoots himself, choosing suicide over the consequences of surrendering to justice. In the final scene of the movie, we see Jean about to marry his childhood love Marguerite and become a stepfather to her children. The tragic, doomed figure of the novella by Michel Verne, thus wins the happiness due to him, at least in the film version.

A scene from Michel's 1916 movie of *La Destinée de Jean Morénas*.

The Character of Pierre Morénas

Jean's brother Pierre, as depicted by Michel Verne in both the novella and the movie, is far from being an unvaryingly, stereotypical wicked person. The portrayal of his character is more complex and nuanced than that. As a youth, Pierre is, admittedly, prone to get into all sorts of fights and scrapes, and likes to carouse, drink and boast. Yet deep down, he is a loving son and brother, though it is Jean who is more dedicated to his mother on a day-to-day basis. Pierre also yearns to leave the narrow confines of his native village in the mountains, and become rich.

He thus disappears suddenly without explanation, but returns some years later after dark, having become destitute, to attack and rob his Uncle Sandy at the inn. He then flees the scene of the crime, not realizing that his uncle has succumbed to his injuries, that Jean has been falsely convicted for murder, and that his mother has later died of a broken heart. When Pierre returns to the village a year later and discovers the horrific consequences of his attack, he feels deep remorse for the unintended, tragic outcomes of his actions, including the imprisonment of his innocent brother. He therefore seeks to make amends to Jean by helping him to escape, though without revealing his identity.

Yet Pierre is ultimately a weak, selfish, cowardly, flawed character. He does not, ultimately, ever confess to his crime, and later re-offends through his attempted murder of the solicitor. He also allows Jean to return to the penal colony following the latter's false confession, at the end of the story. In the film, Pierre is a similarly morally ambiguous character.

Yet in *Pierre-Jean,* the character of M. Bernardon—thought he has, we are told, committed minor offences in his youth—is an essentially virtuous, admirable character.[3]

Narrative Technique

Despite these significant differences in plot, both literary versions have a similar narrative structure and use similar techniques of narration. Both versions employ, for example, the narrative technique of flashback. The story begins in both cases with the visit of Bernardon to the penal colony, but the narrative later travels back in time to

---

3.   For a detailed, authoritative discussion of this and other works by Michel Verne, and his career as both writer and film-maker, readers are referred to the seminal 2001 article by Brian Taves, "The Novels and Rediscovered Films of Michel (Jules) Verne," in the *Journal of Film Preservation,* No. 62 (April 2001), 25-39.

explain how the central character came to be a convict in double chains. The story then returns to the present moment. In *Morénas,* following the departure of Bernardon after his initial visit to the prison, the omniscient third-person narrator takes the reader back in time to the childhood and youthful upbringing of the eponymous hero, and recounts the tragic sequence of events which have led him to where he is today. This flashback sequence (Chapter 4) concludes with Pierre ruminating on how he might make reparation to his brother Jean for his unjust imprisonment. This gives the reader the first strong hint that Pierre and Bernardon are one and the same. In sum, this key retrospective sequence is longer and more complex in *Morénas* than in *Pierre-Jean.* In the latter version by Jules Verne, there is a much briefer flashback towards the very end of the story, in which Bernardon explains to Pierre-Jean the connection he has with him, and his reasons for coming to his rescue.

It is, essentially, the major storyline differences between both flashbacks which strongly differentiate the plot of these two versions. The other significant plot difference lies in the account of what happens to the escapee after breaking free from prison, especially the tragic fate of Jean Morénas as opposed to the happier ending for Pierre-Jean.

The film version of *Morénas* remains, as we have seen, largely faithful to the plot of Michel's retelling, except in its avoidance of a tragic destiny for Jean Morénas in the closing frames. However, in contrast to the novella, the film's narration largely follows a linear, chronological order, apart from a brief flashback which shows some of the characters playing together as children, and explains how they came to discover the secret passage at the inn. In the film, therefore, the story begins, not in the penal colony, but with Jean and Pierre as young men living at home with their mother, the story moving on gradually to the murder of Uncle Sandy, the incarceration of Jean, Pierre's visits to him in disguise as Bernardon, the action-packed escape, the return to Sainte-Marie-des-Maures and the dramatic ending at the inn.

Linguistic Expression and Themes

Having compared and contrasted the plot of the two literary versions and of the film, let us briefly examine some of the similarities—and differences—in the language use and themes in the respective versions by Jules Verne and his son Michel.

Much of the language and content of the early chapters of *Pierre-Jean* has been incorporated wholesale by Michel Verne into *Morénas*. These are the chapters dealing with the conditions at the penal colony, the visits of Bernardon to the convict at the prison, and the dramatic escape. Michel Verne thus transfers much material from his father's original story into his own version, often leaving the linguistic expression largely unchanged. There are, however, slight, subtle variations in the language used by Michel to express almost identical content to that of his father in these scene-setting chapters. Michel also rearranges some of the content.

Examples of very similarly phrased passages include the following from *Pierre-Jean*:

> For the past several months now, not a single sound of cannon fire raising the alarm to signal an escape bid, had occurred to plunge the port of Toulon into a state of terror…
>
> It was not as though a rousing love of freedom had somehow weakened within the heart of the condemned prisoners, though some inexpressible loss of hope and courage seemed indeed to have weighed down their chains and made them all the heavier… several prison guards, who had been found guilty of negligence and treason, had been dismissed from guarding this community of chain gang prison slaves, and it had become a sort of point of honour amongst the replacement prison guards to be more severely vigilant…
>
> In the month of September, a rich, horse-drawn carriage in fine style stopped outside the rear admiral's private mansion; a thirty-five year old man stepped down from the coach. This was M. Bernardon, a wealthy merchant who had only recently established himself in business in Marseilles. (Chapter 1)

The corresponding passages from Michel Verne's *Morénas* read as follows:

> That day—towards the end of the month of September, already a very long time ago—a sumptuous carriage stopped outside the Vice-Admiral's private mansion which overlooked the central square of Toulon. A man of about forty years of age, well-built,

but somewhat coarse and common in appearance, alighted from this carriage, and arranged for certain documents to be conveyed to the Vice-Admiral... "The gentleman to whom I have the honour of speaking is indeed M. Bernardon, the well-known Marseilles-based ship-owner, is that correct?"... for several months now, the cannon-fired alarm signal had not sounded in the port of Toulon.

It is not as though the dedicated love of freedom had weakened in the hearts of the prisoners, but despondency seemed to have weighed down their chains and made them heavier. As a number of prison guards, found guilty of negligence or treason, had been dismissed from the penal colony, it was a point of honour among the remaining guards to be all the more harsh and wary in keeping watch over the prisoners. (Chapter 1)

The ages of Bernardon and the convict differ slightly in both versions: they are aged thirty-five and thirty, respectively, in *Pierre-Jean;* forty and thirty-five in *Morénas.* Bernardon's past life, his present physical appearance, and his length of time as an established, successful businessman, are also markedly different in both stories. In *Pierre-Jean,* for instance, Bernardon and the convict are not brothers. Furthermore, in *Pierre-Jean,* the wealthy merchant

... had only recently established himself in business in Marseille. [He] seemed older than the age indicated by his Birth Certificate; the suffering of his early years could still be plainly read on his brow... his bravery and determination had long ago vanquished the cruel tricks of fate... his mind held scorn for the biases... of this world... he had a cold mistrust of his fellow man... he sought solitude... (Chapter 1)

In *Morénas,* on the other hand, Bernardon is "... a man of about forty years of age, well-built, but somewhat coarse and common in appearance..." (Chapter 1) In sum, the Bernardon of the original version is a finer though less complex character, with a completely different life story, than his counterpart in Michel Verne's retelling.

Social Commentary: The Dickens Connection

Laurent Sudret has pointed out the Dickensian influences which are evident in some of Jules Verne's writings, referring in particular to the social commentary in Verne's "Irish" novel *P'tit Bonhomme* (1893), a title which literally means "*Little Fellow*," but which has been variously published in its English rendering under the titles *Foundling Mick; The Extraordinary Adventures of Foundling Mick* and *A Lad of Grit*.[4] This novel is thus referred to hereinafter, for convenience, as *Foundling Mick*.[5] In *Pierre-Jean*, Verne offers a strong denunciation, and detailed description, of the cruel *régime* of the Toulon penal colony, and of the poverty-stricken existence of tenants such as Bernardon's elderly mother. These instances of social commentary—an essential part of both versions—have echoes of some of the novels of Charles Dickens, such as *Little Dorrit* and *Great Expectations,* the former novel dealing with the Marshalsea debtors'sprison, the latter featuring the convict Magwitch.[6] Similarly, in *Morénas*, and in many of the passages taken from *Pierre-Jean,* the third-person narrator, and the character of Bernardon, both regularly reflect on the horrendous conditions in which the convicts are incarcerated, as in the following passage from *Morénas*:

> Convicts of all ages and all kinds are shamefully muddled together. This deplorable crowding into one place, of very different individuals, can only lead to hideous corruption, and, indeed, the contagion of evil wreaks its devastating effects amongst these poisoned hoards.... Their labors... would not cease until eight in the evening. The convicts would then be brought back to their prisons where, during a few hours of sleep, they would finally be at liberty to forget

4. Laurent Sudret. "P'tit Bonhomme, l'hommage de Verne à Dickens." *Bulletin de la Société Jules Verne*. Vol. 13, no. 1 (2007), 1-13.

5. Readers who are interested in further exploring Verne's "Dickens-themed" literature are advised to read the Royal Irish Academy's 2008 republication of the original translation of Verne's 1893 novel set in Ireland during the Great Famine, *The Extraordinary Adventures of Foundling Mick*, to which I have contributed an afterword, "Translating *Foundling Mick*," and to which William Butcher has written an Introduction.

6. See Charles Dickens, *Little Dorrit* (London: Chapman and Hall, 1850), and *Great Expectations* (London: S.H. Goetzel, 1863).

their grim destiny.… [The prisoners who try to escape] can also get a whipping and may be placed in double chains… Nothing is beyond the realms of possibility… for men who thirst to regain their freedom.…

The requested workmen… urged on by the abuse which was hurled at them by the warrant officers, and often, also, by the fearsome, intimidating canes with which they struck the prisoners… were hitched to heavily-loaded carts; others carried heavy planks on their shoulders, piled up and cleared away timber, or dragged along ships through pulling on tow-lines.…

Before him [M. Bernardon] there unfolded a singularly distressing scene, apt to move any charitable soul. (Chapter 1)

In sum, a central theme of both versions is a stinging indictment of the penal system, whose scenes of debasement are vividly brought to life on the pages. Given that so many of Jules Verne's *Voyages Extraordinaires dans les Mondes Connus et Inconnus* (*Extraordinary Journeys into the Known and Unknown Worlds,* hereinafter referred to as *Extraordinary Journeys*) have been successfully adapted for stage and screen—and lend themselves wonderfully well to a visual medium—it is not surprising that Verne literature is characterised by detailed visual, cinematic descriptions of scenes and events. Both of the stories discussed here are thus strongly visual in their evocation of the penal colony, the sea, the Provençal countryside, villages and architecture, and contain similar references, throughout, to harrowing "tableaux," "vistas," "scenes," "depictions," "colors," "palettes," "canvases" and "frames." For instance, we read in *Pierre-Jean,* the following impressions made on Bernardon by the awful sights at the Toulon prison, in a passage which borrows from the lexical field of portraiture:

Before him was displayed this harrowing scene, framed by the justice system, upon which was depicted in a sad light the debasement and corruption of human passions! Because terrible fate had met with nothing but dreary colors on the palette and canvas of crime! But the uneasy visitor did not stop to dwell on the entire tableau… (Chapter 2)

There are parallels between *Pierre-Jean* and *Foundling Mick,* both by Jules Verne, in their poignant depiction of the effects of unscrupulous landlordism; in the former work, Pierre-Jean meets

> an old woman… weeping alone in a corner, and wringing her arms with despair. Pierre-Jean wished to know the cause of her great sorrow. [She explains that] "one misfortune after another has come to build up on my head; taxes have increased, bad harvests have come to pass, and unless I can come up with the sum of fifty francs, the agents of the law are going to seize and sell off my humble, dilapidated thatched cottage!" (Chapter Five)

This scene has strong echoes of the merciless casting out onto the roadside of the MacCarthy family of County Kerry—including their elderly, dying grandmother—in *Foundling Mick.*

Themes of Filial Devotion

Both Pierre-Jean and Jean Morénas are dutiful, loving sons who mourn the passing of their mother. The former has the following conversation with Bernardon: "That poor, good woman who was my mother," replied the convict with great sadness, "don't say any more to me about her! She is dead!… I've been working very hard because I want to save up enough money to buy a proper grave for [her]." (Chapter 3)

Pierre-Jean is grateful when informed by Bernardon that his mother "has been buried beneath a beautiful marble headstone… with green trees." (Chapter 3) Similarly, when Morénas escapes, he decides that "to see his village once again, to kneel down at his mother's grave… this is what he must do at all costs." (Chapter 8)

Light and Darkness

In both versions, as in the film, there are striking visual contrasts between light and darkness, especially in the final chapter of *Morénas,* the concluding paragraphs of which combine the lexical field of framed images with that of brightness and shadow, which seems to be a metaphor for other contrasts in the story, between happiness and sadness, setting in relief Jean's despair and Pierre's good fortune:

The door, which was wide open, outlined a dark rectangular vista which Jean gazed at passionately. Against this dark background was etched for him the distinct contours of a bittersweet portrait: underneath the unforgiving glare of a deep blue sky, on a sun-scorched quayside, there came and went men carrying heavy loads, their feet weighed down with irons… But above them shone a dazzling image: the image of a young woman who held a little child in her arms… Jean, his eyes riveted to this image, disappeared into the darkness. (Chapter 9)

Conclusion

In sum, this comparison of *Pierre-Jean* with *Morénas* (the novella and the film version) shows what a competent storyteller Michel Verne was in his own right, in both the literary and cinematic genres. Though he found his inspiration in writings which were the work of his father, he was able to remould this influential material into new and original artistic creations of his own. In the novella and film discussed here, he has proved adept at offering an exciting and suspenseful tale of adventure, crime and mystery, which keeps the reader/viewer on the edge of their seat throughout. The literary and film output of Michel Verne merits continued translation, republication and scholarly investigation as part of a new Verne *renaissance*—this time in favour of Verne *fils*.

PIERRE-JEAN

Chapter I

For the past several months now, not a single sound of cannon fire raising the alarm to signal an escape bid, had occurred to plunge the port of Toulon into a state of terror; the convicts, now subjected to much closer and much more effective surveillance, inevitably fell at the first hurdle during their attempts to escape, and the most daring among them retreated when confronted with insurmountable obstacles.

It was not as though a rousing love of freedom had somehow weakened within the heart of the condemned prisoners, though some inexpressible loss of hope and courage seemed indeed to have weighed down their chains and made them all the heavier. Moreover, several prison guards, who had been found guilty of negligence and treason, had been dismissed from guarding this community of chain gang prison slaves, and it had become a sort of point of honour amongst the replacement prison wardens to be more severely vigilant in their surveillance and investigations. The superintendent of the penal colony was mightily self-congratulatory on this outcome, without, for all that, allowing himself to be complacently lulled into a false sense of security; in Toulon, prison escapes are easier and occur more frequently than in any other port; there were thus every grounds for fearing that this possibly feigned period of calm might not be concealing some secretly hatched plan or other.

It is a feature peculiar to employees of the administration and execution of justice to imagine that, when no crime is being committed, it will nevertheless shortly reoccur; so, when they are not in pursuit of criminals, they must keep a close watch on them, and they feel obliged, in the absence of wrongdoing necessitating repression, to argue that there must be a criminal conspiracy of silence.

In the month of September, a rich, horse-drawn carriage in fine style stopped outside the rear admiral's private mansion; a thirty-five year old man stepped down from the coach. This was Monsieur Bernardon, a wealthy merchant who had only recently established himself in business in Marseilles.

This man had a serious face, and seemed older than the age indicated by his Birth Certificate; the suffering of his early years could still be plainly read on his brow, prematurely furrowed as it was by a number of wrinkles; his bravery and determination had long ago vanquished the cruel tricks of fate; his mind held scorn for the biases and prejudices of this world, and he freely shook the hand of the mighty and the humble alike, with equal sincerity, provided they were honest in their greatness or humility!

M. Bernardon was a self-made man who had single-handedly accumulated his fortune; from humble origins, he had risen to a high rank in society; in Marseilles, he was surrounded by the esteem and respect of noble people, and his network of contacts had put him in communication with important figures of society.

Nevertheless, his youthful struggles against misfortune had left him with a cold mistrust of his fellow man; he sought solitude, by means of which he and his family held themselves at a reserved distance, with the result that his business contacts had never developed into social connections. His departure had thus been quiet and without ostentation or haste; he had come to Toulon on the pretext of a piece of mundane family business.

An urgent letter of introduction secured his admission to the home of the rear admiral, who greeted him in a warm and friendly manner and asked him to let him know the purpose of his visit.

"Sir," replied the visitor from Marseilles, "what I have to make of you is a very simple request."

"And what is that?"

"I should like to make a minute and thorough visit of inspection to the penal colony here at Toulon."

"Sir," replied the rear admiral, "your letter of introduction from the chief of police was completely unnecessary; a man of your standing has no need for these official, diplomatic testimonials of his worth, to allow him to pass from one place to another."

M. Bernardon bowed, and, thanking the rear admiral for his kindness and helpfulness, asked him what were the necessary procedures to be followed.

"Nothing could be simpler, sir; please be good enough to present yourself before the rear admiral of the Marine administration, and your wishes shall be granted."

From *Clovis Dardentor* (1896).

M. Bernardon took his leave of the admiral, had himself conducted to the Marine rear admiral's quarters, and was immediately permitted to enter into the naval dockyard. He wished to immediately put his visit to good use, and was brought by an orderly to the superintendent of the penal colony, who graciously placed himself at his visitor's disposal. The Marseilles businessman thanked him but expressed a wish to be alone.

"Please proceed as you wish, sir," replied the superintendent.

"May I be allowed to speak with the convicts?"

"That's perfectly in order, sir; the sergeants have already been notified. I'm presuming that what brings you here today is an intention to do some act of benevolent goodwill?"

"Yes, sir," M. Bernardon replied, without an instant's hesitation.

"We are in the habit of receiving visits of this nature," the superintendent replied. "The government quite rightly requested that improvements be made to the regulatory system of the penal colonies, and you can believe me when I tell you that the convicts' lot has already undergone significant changes."

The visitor from Marseilles bowed.

"There is a severe type of justice which is very difficult to maintain in these type of circumstances; and while we mustn't overstep the mark in enforcing the full rigors of the law, we must be careful of these ultramodern philanthropists who forget the crime when they see the punishment! What's more, we know that there has to be a happy medium when enforcing justice without bias."

"Your sentiments do you great honour," replied M. Bernardon, "and if my observations can be of any interest to you, it will give me great pleasure to discuss these matters with you."

And upon these words, the two men took their leave of each other, and the Marseilles visitor proceeded onwards towards the penal colonies.

The military port of Toulon consists mainly of two enormous polygon-shaped constructions, the northern side of which leans against and supports the quay; one of these polygons, known as the *New Dock*, is located to the west of the second one, known as the *Old Dock*. The sides of these vast enclosures, which are virtually extensions of the city's fortifications, constitute types of barriers wide enough to support long buildings such as the machinery workshops, the military barracks or the special Navy stores. Each of these polygon-shaped docks has, in its southern part, a sufficiently wide opening to allow the passage of high vessels. These beautiful enclosures could easily have been a sort of floating dock, but for the unvarying level of the Mediterranean, which is not subject to significant tidal flows, and which thus made it pointless to close them up. The *New Dock* is bounded to the west by a number of stores and by the artillery depot, and, to the south, at the right-hand side of the entrance facing out onto the small harbour, by penal colonies.

The penal colony consists of two buildings which are joined at a right angle to each other; the first one, which is in front of the steam engine workshop, is exposed to the South; the other faces the *Old Dock* and is extended by the barracks and the hospital; and, independently of the three halls within these structures are three "floating prisons." The latter prisons accommodate those convicts who are serving fixed prison terms and who are due for eventual release, whereas the prisoners serving life sentences are locked up within the cells of the main buildings.

If there is one place in which everybody should not be equal, it is surely these penal colonies; the prison system, by virtue of its gradated diversity of punishments, which are determined by the degree of perversity of the criminal mind, ought to have distinctions in caste and rank! Yet convicts of every description, of all ages, serving all types of sentence, are shamefully mixed together, and from such an appalling amassment, there can result only the most hideous corruption; crime is a contagious infection which wreaks danger and devastation amongst these blighted hordes, and the attempted remedies of the justice system become of no use once evil has permeated the blood and mind.

As can be seen, the prisons are banished to the extreme end of the naval dockyard and to a location as far away as possible from the city.

At that time, the penal colony of Toulon contained close to four thousand convicts; of these, three thousand prisoners, assigned to fatigue duties, worked in such areas as port management, shipbuilding, artillery, general stores, hydraulic construction and non-military building activities; others, who had been unable to secure a place in any of these several major divisions, served in the port, engaged in such tasks as ballasting, removal of ballast, towing of vessels, cleaning and clearing of pits and sewers, transport of sludge and refuse, unloading of

From *Mathias Sandorf* (1885).

timber used for the construction of masts and for other building, and so on, while others still were nurses, or patients, special employees, or convicts locked in double chains because they had attempted to escape at some point.

The clock of the naval dockyard had just rung half-past midday as M. Bernardon made his way towards the polygon-shaped docks; the port was deserted; the convicts, who had left their cells at sunrise, had been working at their diverse occupations until half-past eleven; the ringing of the bell had then recalled them to their respective prison cells; each of them had been given a piece of bread of nine hundred and seventeen grams, or three hundred grams of sea biscuit, as well as forty-eight centiliters of wine. The convicts who were serving life sentences had gone back up to their bench, and the henchmen guarding them had immediately chained them to their seating place, whereas those prisoners serving specific terms could move freely around the entire length of the hall. At the sound of the sergeant's whistle, they had squatted down on their knees around mess-tins of soup which, the whole year round, was made from dried beans. Such was their ordinary daily routine, and these unfortunate prisoners were entitled to their ration of wine only on days of hard labor.

Duties were to be resumed at one o'clock and had to continue until finishing time which was at eight in the evening; the convicts were then returned to their cells, and had to try to get some sleep either on the floor amongst the squashed masses in the floating prisons, or on camp beds on the ground in the land-based prisons, with no other protection against the cold, or relief from the hardness of their "bed," than a tattered strip of grey wool of a coarse fabric.

Chapter II

The convicts were not due to return to their work for another half an hour. M. Bernardon availed himself of their absence to walk round the quays, studying the physical layout of the port and the arrangement of its buildings, the vessels sheltered beneath their covered docks, the immense shells imprisoned within the careening docks, heavy pieces of cast-iron equipment piled up beneath the cranes; but he paid merely scant attention to all of these wonders of industry. Most probably, he was in need of certain details concerning the private lives of the convicts, for he approached one of the overseeing sergeants and said to him:

"Sir, what time are the prisoners due to come back here to the port?"

"At one o'clock," the guard answered.

"Are all of them assigned, without distinction, to the same tasks?"

"Not at all; under the supervision of specialised foremen, there are some among them who work within particular industries; and there are some excellent workmen to be found in the locksmithing and ironmongery workshops, or in the workshops of ropemaking or in the casting and smelting works in foundries, which all require practical skills and knowledge."

"How much can they earn?"

"That depends; they are paid either by the daily hours worked, or according to the particular task done; a day's work can earn them

From *Mathias Sandorf.*

between five and twenty centimes; but if they're paid according to the task, and depending on their skill and speed, they can sometimes make up to thirty centimes."

"And this modest sum," the Marseillais eagerly and anxiously asked, "does it manage to improve their lot?"

"It's enough for them to buy tobacco because, in spite of the official no-smoking rule, the powers that be unofficially turn a blind eye to the prisoners smoking; and for a few centimes also, they sometimes get portions of stew or vegetables."

"Do the convicts serving life, and the fixed-term convicts, all benefit from the same salary?"

"The pay is the same for everybody; but the fixed-term prisoners get a one-third bonus which is kept aside for them until they've served their sentence; they're then given that amount, so as not to be completely destitute when they get out of prison."

"I understand," said M. Bernardon, and he sighed deeply.

"My goodness, sir," replied the sergeant, "they're not all that badly off, and if they weren't causing the severity of their punishments to be redoubled through their misdemeanors or escape bids, well then, as far as their well-being is concerned, they'd be less to be pitied than a whole crowd of workers in the cities!"

This man, hardened to the sight of suffering, called that "well-being"!

"A lengthening of their sentence," asked the visitor from Marseilles, in a tone of voice somewhat broken by his distress, "isn't that, then, the only punishment inflicted on them in the case of an escape?"

"No! There are also the beatings and the double chains!"

"Beatings?" repeated M. Bernardon.

"Which consist of the application of between fifteen and sixty lashes on the shoulders with a tarred rope!"

"And is any chance of fleeing impossible for a convict who has been put in double chains?"

"Just about impossible, indeed," the sergeant replied. "In those cases, the convicts are chained to the foot of their bench, and never get to go out. Which makes it rather difficult to escape!"

"So it's when they're in the middle of their labors that they have the best chance of escape."

"You bet! The pairs of chained convicts, though supervised by a henchman guard, have a certain freedom of movement required by the work, but some of those fellows are so adept, that despite active surveillance, in less than five minutes, the strongest chain can be cut. When the key tethered to the chain's ball is too strong, they keep the ring which surrounds the leg and break the first link of their chain. Lots of the convicts are employed in the locksmith workshops, where they can easily get hold of the materials they need; often, the wrought iron identity plate bearing their number is sufficient for their purposes. If they manage to get their hands on a watch spring, the cannon-fire alarm very quickly booms and roars! When all is said and done, they have a thousand wiles up their sleeves; there was once a prisoner who sold twenty-two of these trade secrets to avoid a whipping!"

"But where can they hide their tools?"

"Everywhere and nowhere. One particular convict had managed to cut slits under his armpits and had slipped little pieces of steel into gaps between his flesh and bone. Recently, I confiscated, from one prisoner, a straw basket which had tiny, hardly visible files and saws concealed in every twig! Nothing is impossible, my good sir, to men whose names are Petit, Collonge or the Count of Saint Helena!"

At this moment, the clock sounded one; the sergeant said goodbye to M. Bernardon and returned to his station.

"Hope and justice!" the businessman said to himself. "But suppose I fail! Good God! Beatings! And the double chain!"

The convicts were now coming out of the prison, some on their own, others chained together in pairs, under the watchful supervision of one of the guard henchmen. The port once again resounded with the sound of voices, the ringing out of irons, and the threats of the "rozzers" or "bluebottles," those low-ranked guards of the penal colony. All of this made a painful impression on M Bernardon, and so as not to display excessive urgency in visiting these unfortunates, he directed his steps towards the artillery depot.

There he found an official displayed notice, of the type to be found in all such prison communities, setting out the penal code of the prison colony.

> The following types of offenders are subject to punishment by the death sentence: all convicts who strike an agent of the law, who kill one of their fellow prisoners, who revolt, or instigate a revolt. The following offence is punishable by three years of double enchainment: attempts at escape by convicts serving life sentences. Fixed-term prisoners who commit the same crime will receive an additional three years of incarceration, and all convicts who steal a sum in excess of five francs will be given an additional prison term to be determined by a judge.
>
> The following types of offenders will be subjected to a beating: any convict who files through his irons, or who employs any attempted means of escape; any convict on whose person shall be found attempts at disguise; who steals a sum less than five francs, who becomes inebriated, who

indulges in gambling activities, who smokes in the port or adjoining areas, who attempts to sell or damage his ragged clothing, who writes letters without authorization, on whose person shall be found a sum not greater than ten francs, who beats up a fellow prisoner, who refuses to work, or who displays insubordination.

Having read these regulations, the visitor from Marseilles remained thoughtful, but was torn from his state of dejection by the arrival of the galley slaves. The port was bustling with activity; work was being allocated at every point of the work areas. Here and there, the drunken voices of the foremen were making themselves heard:

"Ten pairs of convicts for Saint-Mandrier!"

"Fifteen single (non-double chained) prisoners for the rope-making workshop!"

"Ten pairs of convicts needed aloft, for the masts!"

"A reinforcement of six red-caps for the basin!"

The pairs of convicts whose presence was thus requested made their way to their designated workplaces, spurred on by the insults of the sergeants, and even more often by their fearsome cudgels and batons. The visitor from Marseilles observed them closely, and, in particular, tried to discern their prisoner number. Some were harnessed to heavily laden carts; others transported upon their shoulders heavy planks of timber and lumber, piling up and clearing away the wood to be used for construction, while others towed, with cords, the vessels from which weapons had been removed, yet all the while, the sun beat down upon them its punishing rays of burning heat.

The convicts were all identically dressed in a cap made of a rough red material, a waistcoat of the same color and a trousers of rough grey canvas; the prisoners serving life wore a green woollen cap, and were assigned to the most arduous, roughest tasks in the absence of any particular skills on their part; prisoners who were particularly mistrusted because of their depraved instincts or previous escape bids, wore a green cap surrounded by a wide red edge. The completely red cap denoted the prisoners serving fixed terms, and it was upon these that M. Bernardon now focused his anxious, searching observation. Attached to the cap was an iron plate bearing the registration number of each convict.

Some of the convicts, chained together in pairs, trailed irons weighing between eight and twenty-two pounds; the chain which rose from the foot of one of these prisoners rose upwards to his belt to which it was attached, and came back down to attach itself to the belt and foot of his fellow. These unfortunates were jokingly referred to as *the Knights of the Garland*! The others, uncoupled, carried only a ring and a half-chain weighing nine or ten pounds, or even a single ring known as a foot-binding, weighing between two and four pounds. Some particularly fearsome galley slaves had their foot manacled in a small strap, an iron fitting of triangular shape, which, tethered to each of his extremities, and around the leg, was specially fortified so as to resist any attempt at breaking it.

M. Bernardon, asking questions, sometimes of the convicts, at other times of their henchmen guards, travelled round observing the various jobs being done at the port. Sometimes a question would come to his lips, but he did not dare to ask it; he was clearly trying to recognise one of these unfortunate prisoners, and was inwardly racked by burning impatience.

Before him was displayed this harrowing scene, framed by the justice system, upon which was depicted in a sad light the debasement and corruption of human passions! Because terrible fate had met with nothing but dreary colors on the palette and canvas of crime! But the uneasy visitor did not stop to dwell on the entire tableau; rather, he was searching, amongst this crowd, for somebody who was not expecting him!

The person he sought was prisoner number 2,224; nothing remained of his name or family, indeed, that prisoner had nothing at all left; his only link to the world was these few degrading numbers, which categorized him as belonging to a shameful breed—with what a sad baptismal name the penal colony christens its children!

Despite M. Bernardon's searches, 2,224 seemed nowhere to be found. So the businessman enquired of one of the guards, and asked him if this "number" was in prison, or otherwise detained for some reason.

"Excuse me," the guard replied, "the man you're looking for is heaving at the capstan, aloft in the mast!"

"What kind of man is he?"

"Upon my word, a peaceable man, even though he's one of our *comeback ponies*—a re-offender."

That designation indicated, then, that the convict in question was serving his second period of detention in the penal colony.

"If you want to speak to him," continued the sergeant, "go to the masting machine."

M. Bernardon quickly made his way there, and finally saw 2,224 who was in the process of fitting out one of the tillers. The visitor from Marseilles could no longer take his glance from him, and a moist sadness quickly drowned his watchful eyes.

Chapter III

Number 2,224 was a man of thirty years of age, of sturdy build. He had an honest face which exuded a type of intelligence which seemed honest rather than criminal. A sense of deep resignation could be discerned upon the brow of this man; but this appearance of submission was not one of exhausted mindlessness, for at times, through the dejection in his eyes, there shone forth occasional vivid lights.

Surely this inner strength could be harnessed for the purpose of doing good; the even features of this man were not those belonging to the vocation of crime, and a proper education should inevitably redirect this unfortunate prisoner onto the path of righteousness.

He was tethered in chains to an elderly prisoner who, more hardened and brutish, formed a striking contrast with him. Underneath the melancholy brow of the old convict, guilty thoughts were ceaselessly harvested! What a shameful and hideous connection, which constitutes the immense solidarity of the criminal fraternity! What are the origins of this fatal law which forces good-natured human beings to lose their way through being put in forcible contact with evil-minded others? Why, then, is evil that cancerous worm that gnaws away at human goodness?

The pairs of convicts who were working at this moment were hoisting the lower masts of a newly-launched vessel, and, to bring some type of regular rhythm to their efforts, they were singing the song of the Widow. The Widow is the guillotine—the widow of all those whom she puts to death!

Oh! Oh! Oh! Jean-Pierre, oh!
Wash yourself and cut your hair, oh!
Your barber shall now make you fair, oh!
Oh! Oh! Oh! Jean-Pierre, oh!
The rumbling tumbril take your cares, oh!
The Widow's scythe that reaps and tears, oh!

Such an existence as this! What thoughts! Such a dreary horizon, bounded by the prison and the scaffold!

M. Bernardon patiently waited for the workers to take their break. Then, taking advantage of the rest period now given to them, the pairs of workers began to relax. The older of the two convicts lay down, stretched out at full length, on the ground; the younger prisoner leaned against the foot of an anchor, silent and gloomy.

The gentleman from Marseilles came towards him.

"My friend," said he, in an affectionate tone, "I would like to speak with you."

Number 2,224 moved towards the man who had just addressed him, and the movement of the chain roused the elderly convict from his drowsy stupor.

"Hey there," he said, "will you keep still, or you'll get us nabbed by those sly old foxes of guards!"

"Be quiet, Romain; I wish to speak to this gentleman."

"And I say no, goddamit!"

"Slip me some of the end of your chain!"

"No! I'm keeping my half of the chain firm and tight!"

"Romain! Romain!" said number 2,224 who was starting to get angry.

"Okay, let's gamble on it," said Romain, taking a pack of cards from his pocket.

"That does it," retorted the young convict.

The chain attaching the two convicts consisted of eighteen links of six feet each in length; each man's share of the chain thus contained nine links, from which he could thus benefit from a limited manoeuvre of freedom. The two adversaries were now beginning to square aggressively up to each other, and the issue at stake had laid bare a raging greed. Their language was interwoven with incomprehensible words.

M. Bernardon moved towards Romain.

"I'll buy your share of the chain," he said to him.

"How much is it worth to me?"

The businessman removed five francs from his purse.

"Five smackers!" said the old convict: "Done!" and he sprung forward to snatch the money which disappeared, God knows where, then, loosening his chain links which he held rolled in front of him, he went back to his resting place, and lay down with his back to the sun.

"So what do you want with me?" the young prisoner asked his visitor from Marseilles.

The latter fixed him with an intense stare and then said to him:

"Your name is Pierre-Jean; you served five years in the galleys for aggravated robbery; three years ago you were released at the end of your prison sentence, but a short time later, you were caught re-offending, and sentenced again, this time to ten years in irons."

"That's true!" said Pierre-Jean.

"You are the son of Jeanne Renaud."

"That poor, good woman who was my mother," replied the convict with great sadness, "don't say any more to me about her! She is dead!"

"She has been dead this past two years," added M. Bernardon.

"Well, Sir, I've been working very hard because I want to save up enough money to buy a proper grave for poor Jeanne Renaud."

"She has been buried beneath a beautiful marble headstone," the businessman replied.

"With green trees?"

"Yes, Pierre-Jean."

"Oh! Thank you! Sir... but who are you?"

"Listen closely, and let's be careful not to be seen speaking together for too long. Prepare to flee this prison within the next day or two. You must buy your companion's silence even if it means paying a small fortune. Promise him anything, for I shall honour your promises to him; when you're ready, you'll receive all the tools needed to secure your rescue from this place; if you had those tools any sooner, they could put you in a compromising position. Goodbye, Pierre-Jean!"

The Marseilles gentleman calmly continued his inspection, leaving the convict completely dumbfounded by what he had just heard. His mysterious benefactor went round the depot several times, visited two workshops, and then quickly rejoined his carriage, whose horses quickly transported him back to the hotel.

Pierre-Jean had not yet recovered from his astonishment; how was it that this man knew so much about the different circumstances of his life? What was his reason for speaking to him about his late mother? How had Jeanne Renaud come to have a beautiful tomb beneath a leafy shade of trees? What was the advantage to this stranger of helping him break free from the galleys? Nevertheless, he eagerly seized this opportunity which had just been offered to him, and resolved to make all necessary preparations for his imminent getaway.

He would first of all have to let his companion in chains know of the escape he was contemplating; this was an essential step, because the link which enchained them together could not be broken by one of them

From *P'tit Bonhmme* (*Little Boy*, 1893).

without the other becoming aware of it. Romain might possibly wish to also benefit from this escape bid, thus reducing its chances of succeeding.

The elderly convict had only a further eighteen months in irons, left to serve on his prison sentence. Thus Pierre-Jean, trying to convince him to stay put, pointed out to him that, with such a short time left on his incarceration, he should not take the risk of having his sentence increased; but Romain, who could see nothing but the glittering prospect of money as the final outcome of this affair, would not listen to reason and refused to co-operate with the schemes being suggested imaginatively by his comrade. It was only when the latter spoke to him about the several thousands of francs which could well be waiting for the old man upon his release from the penal colony, that the elderly prisoner stopped turning a deaf ear to his comrade's entreaties and began to come round to Pierre-Jean's way of thinking. The difficulty perceived by the older man consisted in his being assured of the method of payment; following prolonged bargaining and discussion, during which Romain manifested a majestic contempt for all promises or words of honour, it was finally agreed that he would be given some diamonds in advance, which he would undertake to hide in a safe place; as for the remainder of his reward, he agreed to trust Pierre-Jean's honesty, the old man's agreement being sweetened by the promise of interest on the agreed sum, at the going rate.

And so Pierre-Jean began to ruminate on the best means of escape. His task was to leave the port without being seen; he had to escape the watchful, trained eyes of the sentries and guards of the colony. Should he employ outright daring and boldness, or try to be more crafty? Both, perhaps! Once he was out in the open countryside, and before the gendarmerie squads had been alerted, it would be easy to be persuasive towards the country dwellers in soliciting their help, and those among them who could be made more co-operative and happier by the prospect of a bonus, would certainly be unable to resist the enticement of a higher amount of money.

Pierre-Jean considered that to act under cover of darkness, thus, after nightfall, would be advantageous to his plans. He was not serving a life sentence, but, instead of being imprisoned in one of those old ships which are used as floating penal colonies, he was, as an exception to the rule, locked up in the land-based cells; to escape from them was difficult, so the important thing was not to go back to them now. So, the virtually deserted ports offered him some prospect of success, as he could not practicably conceive of leaving the depot by any other means than taking to the sea.

Once he reached dry land, it would be a matter for his mysterious patron to show him the route he would then have to take.

Having been thus led by his thoughts to the need to rely on the unknown, he resolved to await further instructions, and to see whether his protector would, first of all, make good the promises made by Pierre-Jean to Romain. Time thus seemed to go by too slowly because of his state of anxious impatience.

The next day, the man from Marseilles came straight up to him.

"Well?"

"Everything's been agreed, Sir, and if you wish to be of service to me, all will pass off successfully."

"What do you need?"

"I've promised three thousand francs to my comrade as soon as he gets out of prison."

"He shall have them! Also…?"

"But he wants something more definite than a promise, and is asking for diamonds in advance as a down-payment."

M. Bernardon looked around carefully to make sure that he was not being watched, and then dropped his lapel badge at the feet of the elderly convict, who seized it, and somewhere within whose person it instantly disappeared. At the same time, Bernardon handed a bag to Pierre-Jean.

"Here," he said, "is some gold, and a file which is one of the strongest you could lay hands on."

"Thank you, sir. Where should I run to?"

"Over by the village of Notre-Dame-des-Maures, in the mountains."

"Consider it done!"

"When will you leave here?"

"Tonight! I'm going to swim for it!"

"Good! Try to come ashore at the Garonne headland. There you will find the necessary disguises. Good luck, and be careful!"

"And grateful—to you," added Pierre-Jean.

The convicts returned to their work. M. Bernardon, composed and quiet, made a close examination of the work going on in the depot, and spoke at length with two notorious galley slaves who took him to be a distinguished benefactor.

Chapter IV

Pierre-Jean made studied attempts to appear as though he was the most relaxed of prisoners; yet in spite of his efforts, an observant onlooker would have been struck by an unusual degree of agitation on his part. The winds of a love of freedom wafted within his heart, reigniting all of those hopes which had been simmering dormantly underneath the ashes of resignation. He was working now with an unaccustomed zeal, and almost betrayed himself through an excess of willingness to work. To feign a lack of concern or anxiety was the most effective disguise.

In order to distract attention from his absence at that evening's assemblage of all prisoners, he had the idea of having himself replaced by one of his comrades near to his fellow chained convict. One of the convicts known as *chaussettes* (stockings)—so-called because of the light ring which they carried round their leg—who had now only several days left to serve of his sentence in the penal colony, and who was thus unchained to any other prisoner, agreed to co-operate with Pierre-Jean's scheme in return for three gold coins; he agreed to re-attach Pierre-Jean's chain to his own feet, for a few minutes, after it had been broken.

Towards seven o'clock that evening, Pierre-Jean took advantage of a moment's rest period to saw into his irons; thanks to the perfect quality of his file, and despite the high calibre iron of his shackles, he quickly and successfully discharged his task. Shortly before the prisoners returned to their cells, and having seen the *chaussette* replace him in the line-up, he huddled behind a hiding place composed of some pieces of timber.

Not far from where he stood, there was an enormous boiler which was intended for a steam frigate; it had been placed in front of the machinery workshop in order to dry. This enormous tank was placed upon its base, and the opening within the furnaces offered the convict an impenetrable place of shelter; benefiting from an opportune moment, he slipped noiselessly inside, taking with him the end of a wooden beam which he had hollowed out into the shape of a hat, and which he had pierced with holes; he waited.

Darkness began to fall; the clock rang eight, and the convicts, dropping tools, made their way back to their prisons, led by the guards of the colony. The cloud-laden skies deepened the darkness and were thus advantageous to Pierre-Jean's designs. As soon as the depot was completely deserted, he emerged from his hiding place, and, creeping along stealthily and silently, made his way towards the careening basins, as he could not pass by the prison buildings; at the other side of the harbour, the peninsula of Cépet was filling up with the shadows of nightfall. A few sergeants wandered round here and there, so that Pierre-Jean sometimes had to halt his forward march and burrow himself deeply into dark recesses; fortunately, he had been able to sever all his iron manacles, so that his movements were silent and unrestricted.

He finally reached the sea, just below the *New Dock*, though not far from the opening which provided access to the harbour. With his makeshift wooden helmet in his hand, he slipped down a rope, and disappeared without a sound beneath the waves.

When he came back up to the surface, he promptly adorned himself with this bizarre headdress; his head thus became invisible to any prying eyes, while the holes which he had previously pierced in the wooden helmet allowed him to see the direction in which he was swimming; he might have been assumed to be a floating lifebuoy.

Suddenly, a blast of cannon fire reverberated through the air.

"That'll be the closing of the port," he thought.

A second, then a third discharge rang out!

"The alarm cannon fire! They've found out that I've escaped! Here I go!" And Pierre-Jean, carefully avoiding the approaching ships and anchor chains, advanced through the waves of the small harbour, near the Millau powder keg. The sea was somewhat rough, but, being a strong swimmer, Pierre-Jean felt that he had sufficient strength to

From *Little Boy.*

swim a long distance. As his clothing was hindering his progress, he removed and abandoned it, and it floated away; his small bag of gold was fixed securely to his chest.

He got as far as the middle of the small harbour without meeting with any obstruction, and, leaning for support against a mooring, a sort of iron lifebuoy, he carefully removed the wooden helmet which had been protectively disguising him.

"Whew!" he gasped, "this part of the journey is only a picnic compared with what I still have to do; when I get out into the open sea, I won't have to worry about running in to anyone; but I need first of all to get past the narrow bottleneck, and it's there that lots of sailing vessels

From *Clovis Dardentor*.

go from that tower of vast proportions, to the fort of the *Aiguilette*: it's going to be a devil of a job to escape from that lot in those vessels.[1] In the meantime, let me get my bearings, and let's not start involving the devil in all of this, at least while he's still not around."

Pierre-Jean managed to find his bearings with precise correctness, thanks to the landmark of the powder keg of the Goubnin, and to the location of the Saint-Louis fort; he now knew that he had to swim onwards in a straight line, and, so as not to be noticed by anybody on either side of him, he needed to swim in the middle of the channel.

He swam onwards silently, his head covered with the aforementioned apparatus; the wind was becoming more chilly, and, combined as it was with dangerous, ominous noises, it could very well negatively affect the sharpness of his powers of hearing; thus, he remained constantly vigilant and on guard, and, despite the crucial importance to him of swimming clear of the small harbour, he advanced at a slow pace, so as not to lend the false lifebuoy which concealed him, an indiscreet and precarious, suspicious degree of speed.

Half an hour went by in this manner; by his reckoning, his rough estimations, he was coming ever nearer to the channel. Suddenly, to his left, he thought he could hear the sound of oars rowing; he stopped, cocked his ear to listen, and waited.

"Hey there!" somebody shouted from a small boat. "Any news?"

"Nothing new!" replied somebody else, from a sailing boat which was passing to the right of the escaped convict.

"We'll never be able to track him down at this rate!"

"But is it definite that he's escaped by sea?"

"There's no doubt about that! His clothes have been fished up."

"Well in that case, we're running the risk of ending up as far away as the Indies!"

"Go to it, me hearties! Keep rowing strongly."

The boats parted, taking separate directions at that point. Pierre-Jean was being actively pursued. Being now able to benefit from the fact that the search parties in the naval vessels were moving further away from him, he took the chance of swimming with some vigorously

---

1. Verne is here referring to two particular landmarks. The fort of the Aiguilette, a military fort apparently so-called because of its military officers who wore ornamental uniforms, containing cords with metal tips, while the Tour Royale, or Royal Tower, to the east, commanded, oversaw and defended, together with the above fort, entry to the Small Harbour.

long breast-strokes, and thereby progressed rapidly towards the narrow passage, struggling against the waves and the feeling of despair which was intensifying all round him, engulfing him.

"Oh!" he said to himself, "if only I were out in the middle of the ocean!"

Can the horrifying predicament of this poor man, at that moment, be even imagined? The open sea! This represented sure death, yet he willingly would choose that fate over the backbreaking cruelty of the penal colony! What tenacious perseverance! What strength of character can sometimes be found amongst these poor unfortunates! It is a dictum often repeated that this kind of moral and physical energy, applied for the purposes of good, is capable of accomplishing great feats; yes, that may be so, but this is a superhuman strength which thus surpasses nature. In order to produce it within this man or any other person, there has to have been a dreadful yearning for freedom. Throughout the normal peacefulness of daily life, such persons might have remained vain, passive and unfortified. But society had rejected, repulsed these poor unfortunates; they had collided harshly with this repellence on the part of society, and the impact of the crash had left these dejected people with the impression of seeing shooting stars.

From time to time, shouts rang out in Pierre-Jean's ears; the boats were intensifying their search for him throughout the harbour and must necessarily be concentrating their vigilant doom-watch on the narrow channel. Pierre-Jean was still swimming for survival!

"I'll drown before I surrender!" he said to himself.

He could already glimpse the great tower and the Aiguillette fort. Torchlight seemed to course along the shore, like so many stars boding ill fortune; the members of the squads of gendarmerie were ready for action. The fugitive slowed the pace of his breaststrokes and allowed himself to be pushed forward by the waves and by the west wind, which inexorably drove him forward towards the open sea.

A glow of light suddenly illuminated the waves, and Pierre-Jean saw all around him, three or four boats carrying lighted torches; he no longer moved a muscle, as just one false movement could lead to his downfall.

"Hey, over there!"

"Nothing there!"

From *Mistress Branican* (1891).

"Has anyone checked in the Lazaret area?"

"What about the area where the cannons are stored?"

"The Navy have been tipped off."

"So he can't have come ashore."

"That would be impossible!"

"Let's keep searching! Keep going!"

Pierre-Jean allowed himself to breathe again. The search vessels were no farther than sixty feet away from him; he was forced to swim at a right angle to the coast.

"Hold on a minute! What's that down there?" a sailor cried.

"What?" somebody replied.

"That black spot that's swimming!"

"In the middle of our boats?"

"Yes?"

"That's nothing of importance! Some lifebuoy drifting along."

"Well, get it back!"

Pierre-Jean was now on the point of diving underwater. But the sound of a foreman's whistle was suddenly heard.

"Keep going, lads! We've got better things to be doing than fishing back up some piece of timber. Forge ahead!"

And so the boats continued on their journey. The unfortunate escapee began to feel more hopeful, stronger; his ruse had not been discovered! With the return of hopefulness, came an increase in his physical strength.

In the far distance, a massive black shape towered upwards in his line of vision.

"What's that?" he wondered. "The *Balaguier* tower! If I could reach that tower I'd be safe. But where exactly am I at this moment?"

He turned round towards the left and recognized the Fort of Saint-Louis.

"That's definitely the tower! If I could get past the cannon stores, I'd be right out in open harbour. Oh, sweet freedom, sweet freedom!"

Suddenly, he found himself plunged into the deepest darkness. The hazy contours of some unclear shape blocked his view of the fort! It was one of the last boats, which collided with Pierre-Jean. The vessel stopped as a result of the collision and one of the sailors leaned over the side of the boat.

"It's only a lifebuoy!" he declared. "Keep going!"

And so, the small open boat continued journeying onwards. But suddenly, there was a terrible twist of fate! An oar struck the so-called lifebuoy, knocked it backwards, and before the escapee could even think about making himself invisible to his pursuers, his shaved head was exposed to all and sundry above the edge of the boat!

"We've got him!" the sailors shouted to each other. "Come on, lads, let's get to it!"

Pierre-Jean dived underneath the sea's surface, and while the sound of whistles coming from every direction, hailed the different boats which were dotted about throughout the surrounding waters, he swam just below the surface in the direction of Lazaret beach. In doing so, he was distancing himself from the agreed location of the

From *Mathias Sandorf.*

rendezvous with his mysterious benefactor, because the beach in question is situated to the left, upon entering the open harbour, whereas the Cape of Garonne stretches out to the right; but he hoped that this stratagem might deceive his pursuers, that is, by his swimming in the direction which was the least favourable to his successful escape.

Notwithstanding this, the place specified by the stranger from Marseilles had to be reached. So, having swum several strokes in the opposite direction, the escaped convict then began to retrace his original route. The boats were now passing each other, all around him. At every moment, he would plunge underneath the waves so as not to be detected. In the end, his skilful manoeuvres successfully threw his

From *Mathias Sandorf.*

pursuers off the scent; but he still needed to reach dry land and to arrive at the designated meeting point.

Pierre-Jean began to feel weaker; his strength was beginning to desert him; on a few occasions, his eyes would shut involuntarily, and his brain would fill up with dizzying, whirling sensations; several times, his hands would become slack, and his heavy, seemingly weighed-down feet would head straight downwards towards the oceanic abyss. However, providence and the waves seemed to take pity on him, and thus in time, threw him up, unconscious, on the shore of the Cape of the Garonne.

When he recovered consciousness, a man was bending over him, and was giving him to drink, a few mouthfuls of restorative brandy.

"You're safe, you've been rescued," this man told Pierre-Jean. "Dressed in strange clothes, and wearing a wig, you will easily get to Notre-Dame-des-Maures, in the mountains of the Anti. Get going, quickly! I'm going to light a torch and keep watch over the beach; nobody will imagine that you've come ashore at this place."

Well, Pierre-Jean did indeed launch himself forward in the direction which had been pointed out to him. After a certain length of time had elapsed, he fell onto his knees, prayed for his mother, and fled onwards with a hastened step.

Chapter V

The countryside situated to the east of Toulon, which abounds in woods and mountains, and is furrowed with ravines, streams and rivers, presented the fugitive with numerous opportunities for safety through concealment. This terrain, through which he had so often wound his way on past occasions, did not hold any hiding places or retreats which might have been unfamiliar to him. He no longer felt in despair of being brought to complete safety, and his ruminations came once again to dwell upon this generous protector and benefactor, whose motives he could not even guess at. Did this gentleman from Marseilles need an enterprising man, filled with resolve on every occasion, with a courageous heart of steel, whom he had gone to seek out at the penal colony? But Pierre-Jean had made up his mind to refuse to become involved in any underhand activities, and to steer well clear of any unworthy propositions, just as he had fled the convicts's galleys.

By the time he was penetrating the Garonne mountains, it was ten o'clock in the evening. He avoided travelling by the well-worn roads used by many, and would throw himself into pits and undergrowth whenever he would hear the sound of human footsteps or that of an approaching cart ring out in the midst of the silence. He thus employed all of the precautionary instincts of a wrongdoer who is about to attempt to commit a crime; his wariness alone wore an honest apparel. Even though his disguise rendered him unrecognizable, he dreaded the possibility of some over-familiar inspection, and his Provencal clothing might somehow give the impression of being borrowed. Apart from the squads of gendarmes who are on high alert as soon as they hear the warning sound of the alarm cannons, the escaped convict may meet a potentially uncompromising enemy in each countryman encountered; reasons of personal safety and of financial greed lend additional force to the sharpness of their visual inspection of any stranger, and add to the speed at which their legs can carry them and to the strength of their arms. If somebody notices a fugitive, he is recognized as such, for there always remains with him some type of physical or moral infirmity, either because, accustomed to the weight of the convict's irons, he drags his left leg a little, or because the fear of denunciation by informants betrays itself in his face.

From *Michel Strogoff* (*Michael Strogoff,* 1876).

However, Pierre-Jean did arrive, safe and sound, at the Grande-Bastide, a traditional Provencal walled town. He was served a bottle of wine and a slice of bacon in an inn, which he entered with a display of as much confidence as possible. He was careful to pay his bill in large *sols,* a type of coin of that period. Having, as was much-needed by him, eaten and drunk his fill and feeling his energy restored, and fearing the imprudence of yielding to sleep, he once more set off on foot. Having spent some time travelling along the road to Saint-Vincent, he decided, as a precautionary measure, to veer to the right, and, without meeting a single soul, he reached the village of Roubeaux, which, he considered, it would be totally pointless to travel through.

There was even a moment when he thought about fleeing the place of the arranged rendez-vous, as he was still worried about the prospect of some shady dealings being in store for him; but his trust and confidence won the day over his fears, and, travelling back up northwards, leaving Hyères to his right, he returned to the mountains a second time.

Daylight had begun to break; and, from now on, his line of conduct consisted of avoiding being examined closely, not avoiding distant looks, sticking to the main roads, walking straight ahead and with as honest an appearance as possible. With this strategy in mind, he readjusted his wig, and, buttoning his jacket, set off again at a brisk and deliberate, resolved pace.

He had been deeply absorbed in his thoughts for several instants, when he thought he could hear the trot of several horses. He climbed to the top of an embankment in order to be able to observe developments, at a greater distance. The bend in the road prevented him from seeing anything; yet he could not have been mistaken, and resting his ear against the ground, he distinctly registered the sound which had struck him.

At that very moment, and before he even had the chance to stand up again, three countrymen rushed towards him and fell upon him; suddenly, he found himself gagged and his hands tied, and his assailants were forcing him to retrace his footsteps.

Two gendarmes on horseback were at that moment emerging onto the road; they came up close to the countrymen, and one of the policemen questioned them.

"An escaped convict, officer, an escaped convict whom we've just captured!"

"Oh! Oh, indeed! The fellow from earlier tonight?"

"He may well be, but, whether it's him or somebody else, we've got him!"

"You've earned yourselves a generous reward!"

"Well, I do declare, that's not to be sneezed at! His clothes don't belong to the naval prison colony, so they can be given to us, into the bargain."

"Do you need our help?" asked one of the gendarmes.

"Oh, goodness gracious, no, not at all! He's solidly anchored to us, and we'll be well able to bring him back to justice, all the same!"

"That's just as well," replied the gendarme, "because we're following a trail, and this would jeopardize our tour of duty."

"Off you go, then! See you, and good luck!"

The gendarmes continued on their own journey, while the local countrymen set off in the opposite direction. Pierre-Jean felt annihilated and walked with the air of an automaton. Bound and gagged, he was unable to even try to bribe his captors. Once the gendarmes were out of sight, the countrymen, leaving the main road, began to take deserted routes, off the beaten track, and, at the end of a lengthy march, throughout which they did not speak a word to Pierre-Jean, they reached the Gapau River. While they crossed it on a ferryboat, the unfortunate fugitive felt like flinging himself into the waters; but, restrained by the strong hands of his captors, he had no choice but to abandon any notion of a suicide attempt.

As for these countrymen, they too avoided the main roads, and they were soon in deep mountainous territory. Pierre-Jean could not make head nor tail of their manner of proceeding, could make no sense of their actions. These were the Anti mountains. They had turned their back on Toulon and must by now be very close to Notre-Dame-des-Maures. Indeed, the village of Teste des Caneaux soon became visible to them; they went round the periphery of this village and reached the main road.

There was a man on the other side of the road who seemed to be expecting them. Pierre-Jean was led to this man; he turned out to be none other than M. Bernardon. The prisoner wished to make some gesture of communication, but the Marseilles citizen walked in front of them, taking charge of conducting the troupe of travellers to their final destination. The little troupe did not take long to reach a small

From *Un Drame en Livonie* (*A Drama in Livonia*, 1904).

house, located at a short distance from the village of Notre-Dame-des-Maures.

Pierre-Jean was led into a low-ceilinged room in which there was an old woman. M. Bernardon followed him, with the three countrymen, and the fugitive was untied and unbound.

"What do these people want with me? This is a bad business, sir," he said to the Marseilles gentleman.

"These men are loyal in my service," replied M. Bernardon; "if they hadn't pretended to be bringing you back to Toulon, those two gendarmes would have arrested you, and it would have been all over for you!"

Pierre-Jean could no longer understand anything of what was going on. It was indicated to him that he should sit, whereupon M. Bernardon began to speak to him:

"Listen. Three years ago, Pierre-Jean was being released from the penal colony in which he had just completed his sentence, as he had been condemned to five years of penal servitude and hard labor on the galleys. The hour of freedom had finally rung out for him; equipped only with his passport, wearing nylon trousers, a new shirt and an oilskin hat, he left the prison colony and took more or less the same route as you have taken this day.

"His total fortune amounted to about fifty francs, a pitiful nest-egg which he had gradually and painstakingly built up, one coin after another. There had certainly never been any evil intentions in his heart; in a moment of error, he had fallen by the wayside, but his severe punishment, far from corrupting him by placing him in the company of all sorts of villains, had spurred him on to good and serious reflections; he wished to see his elderly mother again, to support her in all of her labors, and to love her with all his heart.

"Thus was his step a swift and joyful one, for it took him far from the penal colony and brought him back, ever closer, to his native region. The only events to attenuate his joy were when he would redden with shame, whenever gendarmes would oblige him to produce, for inspection, that infamous yellow passport which an excessively cruel law forces freed convicts to display upon their person.

"At the end of a long trek, having reached this village of Notre-Dame-des-Maures, he stopped at this very house. Inside this house was an old woman—and that old woman, it is she whom you see before you now! She was weeping alone in a corner, and wringing her arms with despair. Pierre-Jean wished to know the cause of her great sorrow.

"Alas," she said, "my son is far away from me; he travelled over the seas in order to make his fortune and to become a wealthy man, and in so doing, to release me from my life of difficulties and sorrow; but what has happened is that, since his departure, one misfortune after another has come to build up on my head; taxes have increased, bad harvests have come to pass, and unless I can come up with the sum of fifty francs, the agents of the law are going to seize and sell off my humble, dilapidated thatched cottage!"

"It appears that this woman possessed the eloquence of truth mingled with that of tears; the bailiff was indeed likely to arrive at any moment, and throw her out onto the main road!

"Pierre-Jean loved his own mother dearly; Jeanne Renaud, who was also elderly and in difficult circumstances, had perhaps also been in a similar plight of destitution, and the duty of any charitable soul would have been to come to her rescue in her hour of need; Pierre-Jean's only worldly possession at this moment was that sum of fifty francs; yet he gave them to this good woman. Pierre-Jean had done a kind deed; he left that cottage, happy with himself, and feeling a sense of pride in his heart; but, just at that moment, the bailiff entered the thatched cottage.

"As he walked onwards, and not at all regretting his compassionate deed, Pierre-Jean calculated that if he had had one hundred francs, there would now be fifty francs remaining in his possession; fifty very useful francs, both for the completion of his journey and in order to provide for the most essential needs of his and his mother's existence, for his unfortunate mother was poverty-stricken! Furthermore, it would prove difficult to find employment, once any potential employer would discover where Pierre-Jean had come from!

"As it happened, just at that very moment, the aforesaid bailiff, having received full and due payment from the old woman, to whom he had given a receipt confirming discharge in full of her debt through the money handed over by her, passed by the same way as Pierre-Jean as he (the bailiff) returned to his offices.

"I don't know what nefarious inspiration, at that moment, took hold of Pierre-Jean, but, without taking anything else from the bailiff,

From *A Drama in Livonia*.

he took back possession of his fifty francs, neither more nor less, and, reflecting that his kindly action would compensate for the bad one, continued on his way!

"But before he had the chance to be reunited with his mother, and having been reported and pursued for robbery from the bailiff's person, he was once more brought before the Court of Assizes and sentenced to ten years in convict's irons!—The poor man, he was to be pitied, for his elderly mother died soon afterwards, without having gotten the chance to embrace her son!"

M. Bernardon stopped speaking, his account of the facts having been completed; Pierre-Jean felt large tears moistening his eyes. The stranger from Marseilles took the hand of the old woman and placed it in that of Pierre-Jean.

"This is my mother," he told him, "and it is you who saved her! Both of us have prayed for your own late mother!"

Pierre-Jean fell to his knees; M. Bernardon helped him up.

"My friend, this very day we are returning to Marseilles; one of my ships will carry you to the New World. Take this money, which will forever keep you sheltered from financial need! However, you must swear to me that you will work hard."

"I swear I will indeed do so, sir, even if it was for no other reason than to redeem myself in your eyes!"

M. Bernardon shook his hand, with these words:

"You have been, in my eyes, for a very long time, a true gentleman, a man of breeding!"

That very evening, accompanied by the Marseilles businessman and his mother, Pierre-Jean arrived at Marseilles, and, the following day, the three-mast vessel, the *Cérès,* of seven hundred tons, having taken aboard the new passenger it had been expecting, set full sail towards the Strait of Gibraltar.

LA DESTINÉE DE JEAN MORÉNAS (¹).

The Sombre Fate of Jean Morénas.

THE SOMBRE FATE OF JEAN MORÉNAS

Chapter I

That day—towards the end of the month of September, already a very long time ago—a sumptuous carriage stopped outside the Vice-Admiral's private mansion which overlooked the central square of Toulon. A man of about forty years of age, well-built, but somewhat coarse and common in appearance, alighted from this carriage, and arranged for certain documents to be conveyed to the Vice-Admiral, consisting of—other than his visiting card—letters of introduction bearing the signatures of such eminent persons that the audience he requested was immediately granted.

"The gentleman to whom I have the honour of speaking is indeed M. Bernardon, the well-known Marseille-based ship-owner, is that correct?" asked the Vice-Admiral as soon as his visitor had been shown in.

"The very same," replied the latter.

"Please be seated," the Vice-Admiral went on, "and accept my assurances that I am completely at your service."

"I'm very grateful to you for that, Admiral," M. Bernardon thanked him, "but I do not believe that the request which I am about to make of you is one which you would find difficult to treat favorably."

"And what is the nature of your request?"

"Quite simply, I wish to obtain authorization to visit the penal colony."

"Indeed, nothing could be simpler to arrange," agreed the Vice-Admiral, "and it was quite unnecessary for you to procure the letters of recommendation that you have transmitted to me. A man bearing your name has no need of such character testimonials."

M. Bernardon bowed, then, having once again expressed his gratitude, enquired as to the procedures which would have to be complied with.

"There are none whatsoever," was the reply he received. "Go find the Major General, with this note from myself, and your request will be immediately granted."

M. Bernardon took his leave of the Vice-Admiral, was conducted to the Major General and obtained forthwith permission to go into the naval dockyard. An orderly led him to the offices of the Chief Administrator of the penal colony, who offered to accompany him.

The gentleman from Marseilles, though conveying his deep gratitude, declined the offer made to him and expressed a desire to remain alone.

"As you wish, Sir," said the Chief Superintendent, deferring to the visitor's preference.

"So, there's no difficulty in my going round freely inside the penal colony?"

"None at all."

"Nor in my speaking to the convicts?"

"Neither will there be any problem with that. The warrant officers have been notified of your visit and won't place any difficulties in your way. Might I ask, however, your intention in making this visit—which, as it happens, is hardly a very cheery undertaking?"

"My intention…?"

"Yes. Is it purely a question of curiosity, or do you have some other aim in mind… a philanthropic aim, for instance?"

"Philanthropic—precisely," was M. Bernardon's quick, eager retort.

"How wonderful!" the Chief Superintendent exclaimed. "We are accustomed to these visits, which are very favorably looked upon in high places, as the Government is always seeking to establish what improvements might be made to the penal colony system. Many such improvements have already been achieved."

M. Bernardon made a slight gesture of agreement, without replying, and with the air of a man who was not particularly interested in these observations; but the Chief Superintendent, fired with enthusiasm for his topic of discussion, and finding the moment to be especially opportune to a declaration of his principles, did not notice the behaviour of his interlocutor, and, unperturbed, pursued his line of reasoning:

"It's very hard to find a happy medium as far as this matter is concerned. While one mustn't be excessive in the application of the full rigors of the law, it's also advisable to beware of sentimental critics who forget the crime as soon as they see the punishment meted out. However, in this prison, we never lose sight of the fact that justice ought to be moderately and reasonably administered."

"Such sentiments indeed do you honour," replied M. Bernardon, "and if my observations may be of interest to you, it would be a pleasure to discuss my impressions with you, following my visit to this penal colony."

The two speakers then took leave of each other, and the gentleman from Marseilles, bearing a duly authorized pass, proceeded in the direction of the penal colony.

The military port of Toulon consisted principally of two immense polygons, whose northerly side formed a boundary with the quay, and one of which was known as "The New Port," situated to the west of the other, referred to as "The Old Port."[1]

The periphery of these enclosures, which could truly be regarded as actual continuations of the city's fortifications, was marked by barriers wide enough to hold long buildings, machine workshops, barracks, Navy stores, and so on. Each of these ports, which still exist to this very day, contains, in its southern part, a sufficiently wide opening to allow the passage of tall ships. The ports could thus quite easily have served as floating docks, had it not been for the fact that the constancy of the sea level of the Mediterranean, which is not subject to noticeably high tides, had made it pointless to close them.

At the time of the events which are about to be recounted, the New Port was, at its western boundary, adjoined by the warehouse and

---

1. A polygon is defined as a closed plane figure bounded by three or more straight sides that meet in pairs in the same number of vertices, and do not intersect other than at those vertices. Specific polygons are named according to the number of sides they contain, e.g. a triangle, a pentagon, etc. In this context, Verne's use of the term "polygone" seems to refer to the particular shape of the layout or plan of the prison fortifications, or, as defined in *Le Nouveau Petit Robert* (2008), "Polygone formant le tracé d'une place de guerre, d'une fortification" ("a polygon forming the layout of a military area or fortification"), a usage which dates from 1640.

artillery depot, and, to the South, at the right of the entry which opens onto the small harbour, it was bounded by the penal colonies, whose use has since been discontinued. These colonies consisted of two buildings which were joined at a right angle to each other. The first, which was in front of the machine workshop, faced due south; the second faced the Old Port and was extended by the barracks and the hospital. Separately to these constructions, there were three floating prisons, which housed those convicts who were serving fixed-term sentences, while the convicts serving life sentences were confined on *terra firma*.

If there is one place on this earth in which equality ought not to prevail, it is surely the penal colony. The extent of the punishments administered to prisoners ought to involve hierarchies and distinctions of caste and rank, in proportion to the magnitude of the crimes committed and the degree of mental perversity of the individual prisoner. Yet this is far from being the case. Convicts of all ages and all kinds are shamefully muddled together. This deplorable crowding into one place, of very different individuals, can only lead to hideous corruption, and, indeed, the contagion of evil wreaks its devastating effects amongst these poisoned hoards.

At the time when this story begins, the penal colony of Toulon contained close to four thousand convicts, three thousand of whom were employed within the departments of Port Management, Shipbuilding, Artillery, General Stores and Hydraulic and non-military construction, and it was these convicts to whom the most arduous labors were reserved. Those for whom a place could not be found within these five major sections were employed, in the port, on ballasting duties, removal of ballast and the towing of ships, the transport of sediment, and the loading and unloading of military equipment, stores and provisions. Others carried out nursing duties, were special employees, or had been condemned to wearing double shackles because of a failed escape bid.

At the time of M. Bernardon's visit, no incident of this nature had been recorded for quite a long while, and for several months now, the cannon-fired alarm signal had not sounded in the port of Toulon.

It is not as though the dedicated love of freedom had weakened in the hearts of the prisoners, but despondency seemed to have weighed down their chains and made them heavier. As a number of prison guards, found guilty of negligence or treason, had been dismissed from the penal colony, it was a point of honour among the remaining

An orderly accompanied him.

guards to be all the more harsh and wary in keeping watch over the convicts. The superintendent of the penal colony was highly delighted at this outcome, but did not allow himself to be lulled into a false sense of security, because, in Toulon, prisoners escaped more frequently and with greater ease than in any other port-based penal settlement.

The clock of the Naval dockyard was sounding half past midday, when M. Bernardon reached the end-point of the New Port. The quay was deserted. Half an hour earlier, the bell had recalled, to their respective prisons, the convicts who had been at work since dawn. Each of them had then received his daily ration of food.

Those prisoners who were serving life sentences had gone back up onto their bench, where a guard had immediately secured their chains, while those convicts who were serving fixed-term sentences could freely move about throughout the entire length of the room. Upon the whistle-blow of the warrant officer, they had squatted down around their mess tins containing soup which, the whole year round, was made of dried beans.

Their labors would be resumed at one o'clock, and would not cease until eight in the evening. The convicts would then be brought back to their prisons where, during a few hours of sleep, they would finally be at liberty to forget their grim destiny.

Chapter II

M. Bernardon turned the absence of the convicts to his advantage, in order to examine the layout of the port. However, it may be presumed that the sight in question was only of moderate interest to him, because he quickly made it his business to be standing near to a warrant officer, to whom he now spoke without any further ado: "Sir, at what time do the prisoners come back to the port?," he asked.

"At one o'clock," replied the warrant officer.

"And are they all grouped together and put to work, without distinction, at the same jobs?"

"No: there are some among them who are employed within particular industries, under the leadership of foremen; there are some excellent workmen in the locksmiths' workshop, and in the rope-making workshop and foundry, which are all trades requiring particular skills."

"And do they earn a living from this work?"

"Of course."

"How much can they earn?"

"That depends. At the moment, they can earn anywhere between five and twenty centimes for a day's work. A specific task can earn them up to thirty centimes."

"Are they entitled to put these few coppers towards improving their lot?"

"Yes," replied the warrant officer. "They're allowed to buy tobacco, because, despite regulations to the contrary, it's unofficially tolerated that they smoke. For a few centimes, they can also get portions of ragout or vegetables."

"Do the convicts serving life sentences get the same wages as those serving fixed-term sentences?"

"No, the fixed-term prisoners also earn a bonus of one third, which is kept aside for them until they've served their sentence, upon which they receive the full amount of the bonus, so that they won't be completely impoverished when they get out of prison."

"Ah!..." was the only reply made by M. Bernardon, who now seemed to become absorbed in his own private reflections.

"My goodness, sir," the warrant officer went on, "they're not all that badly off. If they weren't themselves increasing the severity of their punishments through their misdemeanors or their attempted break-outs, they'd be better off than a lot of the workmen outside in the cities."

"So, an increased length of sentence," asked the man from Marseilles, whose voice now seemed slightly altered, "is not the only punishment inflicted upon them, in the case of an attempted escape?"

"No. They can also get a whipping and may be placed in double chains."

"A whipping? ..." repeated M. Bernardon.

"Which consists of blows onto the shoulders—anywhere between fifteen and sixty lashes depending on the case—administered with a tarred rope."

"And, no doubt, any type of escape becomes impossible for a prisoner placed in double chains?"

"That's just about right," replied the warrant officer. "Once that happens, convicts are tied to the foot of their bench, and are never allowed to go out. Under those conditions, escape is no easy matter."

"So, it's while they're at work that they are likely to be able to escape most easily?"

"Most probably. The pairs of workmen, even though they're closely watched by a prison guard, do have a certain freedom of movement which is called for by the nature of the work itself, and such is the skill of these people, that, in spite of the keenest and most watchful supervision, the strongest chain may be severed in less than five minutes. When the key fastened into the moveable bolt is too resistant, they hold onto the ring-shaped link around their leg, and cut the first link of their chain. Lots of convicts, assigned to the locksmiths' workshops, have no trouble finding the tools they need, right there in their workplace. Often, the tin plate bearing their prisoner number is sufficient for them. If they manage to get hold of a watch-spring, the alarm cannon very quickly starts to thunder out its signal. At the end of the day, they have a thousand and one little ruses and resources, and there was even one convict who sold us no fewer than twenty-two of these trade secrets, so as to get out of a whipping!"

"But where are they able to hide their instruments?"

"Everywhere and nowhere! There was one convict who had cut slits underneath his armpits, and used to slip little pieces of steel between flesh and skin. Recently, I confiscated from one prisoner, a straw basket, whose every wisp held tiny files and saws which were practically invisible! Nothing is beyond the realms of possibility, sir, to men who thirst to regain their freedom."

At this very moment, one o'clock rang out. The warrant officer bade M. Bernardon good-bye and returned to his duties.

The convicts were, by now, coming out of the penal colony, some singly, others attached together in pairs, under the surveillance of the prison guards. Soon, the port resounded with the noise of voices, the clanging of irons and the threats of the prison warders.

In the artillery store, which he now came upon by chance as he strolled round, M. Bernardon found, affixed to a wall, a proclamation of the Penal Code of this community of convicts:

> The assault, by any convict, of a prison officer; the murder of a fellow convict; revolt, or the instigation of same, shall all be punishable by death;
>
> The following persons shall be punished by three years of double chains: any convict serving a life sentence who shall have attempted to escape from this prison;
>
> Punishable by a three year extension of prison sentence, shall be any fixed-term prisoner who shall have committed the same crime, and by an extended sentence--the length of which shall be determined by judgement of a court--any convict found to have stolen a sum in excess of five francs.

Punishable by whipping, shall be any convict found to have broken his irons or to have used any particular method to procure his escape; on whose person are found disguises of any type; who steals a sum not exceeding five francs; who is found to be under the influence of intoxicating drink; who gambles; who smokes within the port; who sells, or causes excessive wear and tear to, his garments; writes letters without due authorization; on whose person is found a sum of money in excess of ten francs; who beats his comrade; who refuses to work, or who displays any form of insubordination.

Having read this notice, the man from Marseilles remained deep in thought, until he was roused from his reflections by the arrival of a team of convicts. The port was bustling with activity; duties were being allocated at every point. Here and there, the harsh voices of foremen forcefully shouted out their requests:

"Ten pairs of workers for Saint-Mandrier!"

"Fifteen old rags (chaussettes) for the rope-making workshop!"[1]

"Twenty pairs of men to the masts!"

"A reinforcement of six reds for the dock!"[2]

The requested workmen proceeded to their designated workstations, urged on by the abuse which was hurled at them by the war-

---

1. "Fifteen old rags (chaussettes)" : The French word "chaussettes," as employed here in the French-language source text by Jules Verne, as a derogatory appellation given to certain inmates of the Toulon penal colony by their harsh masters (specifically those convicts in chains who wore a metal ring known also as a "chaussette") , literally means "socks" or "stockings," but can also have the pejorative meaning of an "old rag" or "something without importance," as in the French expression "laisser tomber quelqu'un *comme une vieille chaussette*" (my italics). This expression is explained by *Le Nouveau Petit Robert de la Langue Française 2008* as meaning "*comme une chose sans importance*" (p. 408, my italics), i.e. "to drop somebody like an old sock, or an old rag: like something of no value" (my rendering). Thus, at the time in which this story is set, the chained convicts described by Verne, who wore the ring or "chaussette" round their legs, were themselves also pejoratively referred to as "chaussettes," presumably also implying that the convicts themselves were regarded as practically worthless.

2. The term "reds"—or "rouges" as employed in the French original—appears to be a further type of shorthand label used to designate the prisoners of this port-based penal colony who, as described by Verne further on in the body of this second chapter, wore a red prison uniform.

rant officers, and often, also, by the fearsome, intimidating canes with which they struck the prisoners. The visitor from Marseilles carefully observed these "galley slaves" who filed past him.[3] Some were hitched to heavily-loaded carts; others carried heavy planks on their shoulders, piled up and cleared away timber, or dragged along ships through pulling on tow-lines.

The convicts all wore the same prison clothing, consisting of a red tabord or prison uniform, a vest of the same color and grey canvas trousers.[4] In addition, those prisoners who were serving life sentences wore a woolen cap which was completely green in color. Those among them who were lacking in any particular skills were assigned to the hardest labors. Those prisoners who had become particularly notorious objects of suspicion, because of their perverted instincts or escape bids, wore the headdress of a green cap edged with a wide red strip. A completely red cap, adorned by a tin plaque which bore the prisoner number of each convict, was worn by those prisoners serving fixed terms, and it was these particular convicts whom M. Bernardon now studied with the greatest attention.

Some of these convicts, chained together in pairs, wore irons weighing between eight and twenty-two pounds. The chain, going from the foot of one of the pair of condemned men, went up to his belt where it was secured, and from where it went on to be fastened to the belt, and then the foot of, his comrade in chains. These unfortunate

---

3. Verne occasionally uses the term "galérien" to describe the convicts, as an alternative to the word "forçat" meaning "convict" (literally, "galérien" is translated as "galley slave," but , by extension, it has come to be used to refer to convicts generally). I have here given the literal translation/original meaning of "galérien," in order to try to convey the emotive connotations of the French term, which here appears, in Verne's choice of it, deliberately less neutral than "forçat"/"convict."

4. "A red tabord": The original French word used by Verne here is "casaque," which nowadays refers most often to a jockey's blouse, but which, historically, referred to a "tabard" as worn by musketeers among others. *The Collins English Dictionary* (2003: 1638) defines a tabard as "a sleeveless or short-sleeved jacket, especially one worn by a herald, bearing a coat of arms, or by a knight over his armour," and the word dates back to the thirteenth century, coming from the Old French tabart, of uncertain origin. The French equivalent "casaque" dates from 1413, and while its origin is also uncertain, it probably originates from the Turkish word "*kazak*" meaning "adventurer," a name given to horsemen from the Black Sea area in the Middle Ages, and later applied to their clothing. (*Le Nouveau Petit Robert 2008*: 361).

men were jokingly referred to as the *Knights of the Garland*.[5]

Others wore only a single metal ring-shaped link and a half-chain of between nine and ten pounds, or sometimes only the ring-shaped link itself, which was referred to as the stocking or old rag (chaussette), and which weighed between two and four pounds. Certain particularly fearsome convicts had one of their feet shackled into a so-called hammer, a type of triangular horseshoe which, fastened at each of its extremities around the leg and toughened using a special procedure, is resistant to all attempts at breaking it.[6]

M. Bernardon, occasionally questioning the prisoners, at other times, their guards, moved around the port, examining the various labors being undergone. Before him there unfolded a singularly distressing scene, apt to move any charitable soul: and yet, the truth of the matter was that he did not really seem to see what was going on. Without stopping to focus on the entirety of the scene, his eyes darted round everywhere, seemingly registering the convicts one after another, as if, somewhere in the midst of this pitiful crowd, he was looking for somebody who was not expecting his visit. But his protracted search went on in vain, and, at certain moments, the uneasy visitor could not prevent himself from manifesting signs of discouragement.

His walk round the port eventually brought him, by chance, towards the mast.

Suddenly, he stopped and stood stock-still, his eyes riveted on one of the men harnessed to the capstan. From the place where he stood, the visitor could discern the number of this convict, the number 2,224, which had been cut into a tin plaque attached to the red cap worn by all of the fixed-term prisoners.

---

5. In the original, the term used is *Les Chevaliers de la Guirlande*. This mocking label has ironic echoes of *Les Chevaliers de la Table Ronde* (*Knights of the Round Table*), and the noble connotations of "knight" are ironic in their application to these demeaned prisoners. And while "garland" appears to jokingly refer to the chains in which these convicts are shackled, the term "guirlande" was also, in the eighteenth century, a (now disused) nautical term, referring to a wooden part of the stem of a ship (Robert: 1202). Could this nautical association also have some part to play in the application of the appellation "Guirlande" to these prisoners of this nautical penal colony/floating prison?

6. Hammer: The original term is *martinet*, meaning a hammer, and also referring to a small whip or strap once used on children. It is also the name of a type of bird (a "swift" in English) and is a now obsolete word for a type of candlestick.

Chapter III

Prisoner number 2,224 was a thirty-five year old man, well-built: he had an open, honest face, which simultaneously managed to express both intelligence and resignation. This was not, however, the resignation of a brutal lout whose spirit has been crushed as a result of the degrading labors to which he has been subjected, but rather, a thoughtful acceptance of unavoidable hardship, which is, nevertheless, not at all irreconcilable with the survival of a quiet, inner strength, which was evident in the resoluteness of his gaze.

He was chained to an elderly fellow prisoner who, more hardened and brutish, formed a sharp contrast with his younger comrade, and whose despondent brow could harbour only the most despicable thoughts.

The pairs of workers were, at this moment, hoisting the mast of a newly-launched vessel and, in order to provide some rhythm to their labors, they were singing the song of the *Widow*. *The Widow* is none other than the guillotine, the widow of all those whom she[1] puts to death.

> Oh! Oh! Oh! Jean-Pierre, oh!
> Have a wash and cut your hair, oh!
> There's your barber, over there, oh!

---

1. In the original text, the feminine subject pronoun "elle," referring to the guillotine, can normally mean either "it" or "she," depending on the context. In this instance, the French pronoun accentuates the feminine gender here ironically attributed to the guillotine, so I have tried to replicate this effect by using "she" rather than "it," highlighting the "Widow" rather than the impersonal mechanical instrument of execution.

Oh! Oh! Oh! Jean-Pierre, oh!
There's the tumbril! Reap the hay, oh!

M. Bernardon waited patiently until these operations were temporarily suspended, at which point the pair of convicts who were of particular interest to him reaped the benefit of this momentary respite by taking a short rest. The older of the two convicts stretched himself out completely on the ground; the younger, leaning against the fluke of an anchor, remained standing.[2]

The visitor from Marseilles now approached this younger convict, saying: "My friend, I would like to have a word with you."

In order to approach the man who was speaking to him, number 2,224 had to stretch his chain, the movement of which roused the elderly convict from his doze.

"Hey there!" he said, "would you stand still or you'll get us nabbed by the bloody *guard dogs* as I calls 'em!"[3]

"Be quiet, Romain. I want to speak to this gentleman."

"No, I tell you!"

"Draw out a little of your chain at the end of it."

"No! I'm keeping my half fully tightened!"

"Romain! Romain!" said number 2,224, beginning to get angry.

"Okay then! Let's gamble for it," proposed Romain, taking a filthy pack of cards from his pocket.

"Alright then," replied the younger prisoner.

The chain joining the two convicts consisted of eighteen links measuring, in total, six feet. Each prisoner possessed nine of these links, and therefore enjoyed a corresponding freedom of maneuver.

M. Bernardon now went towards Romain. "Let me buy your share of the chain," he offered.

"Can you make it worth my while?"

The businessman took five francs from his purse.

---

2. The fluke—also known as the flue—of an anchor is a flat bladelike projection at the end of the arm of the anchor. As is his wont throughout so many of his works, Verne uses much domain-specific technical terminology and thus shows the extent of his research.

3. Guard dogs: In the original, the convict reprimands his comrade with the words "Que tu vas nous faire serrer par les renards" (literally, the "foxes"), so that his prison guards are deprecatingly referred to by the name of an animal.

"Your name is Jean Morénas?"

"A five-franc piece!"[4] cried the old convict. "Done!"

He seized the money, which disappeared God knows where, then, unrolling his portion of the chain links which he had previously wound up around himself, he returned to the spot from which he had come and lay down with his back to the sun.

"What do you want with me?" asked number 2,224 of the stranger from Marseilles.

---

4. In the original French, the convict uses the term "une thune," which was a slang term for a coin worth five francs.

The latter, meeting his gaze steadily, declared: "Your name is Jean Morénas. You have been sentenced to twenty years in the galleys for murder and aggravated theft. As things stand, you have served half of your sentence."

"That's correct," said Jean Morénas.

"You are the son of Jeanne Morénas, from the village of Sainte-Marie-des-Maures."[5]

"That poor, good woman, my mother!" the prisoner sadly replied. "Say no more to me about her! She is dead!"

"These nine years," said M. Bernardon.

"That's right also. So who are you, sir, that you know so much about my business?"

"What does it matter to you?" was M. Bernardon's retort. "The important thing is what I wish to do for you now. Listen carefully, and let's make sure that we don't spend too much time talking to each other. Prepare to flee this prison within the next two days. Buy your companion's silence. Make him whatever promises are necessary; I can guarantee those promises will be made good. When you're ready, you will receive all necessary instructions. Goodbye for the present!"

The unruffled visitor from Marseille then continued, imperturbably, his inspection of the port, leaving the prisoner dumbfounded at what he had just been told. M. Bernardon went round the naval dockyard several times, visited various different workshops, and shortly returned to his carriage, whereupon his horses carried him away at a full trot.

---

5. The name of this French village from which Jean Morénas originally comes, can be translated as "Saint Mary of the Moors" ("Moors" in the sense of the Moorish peoples).

Chapter IV

Fifteen years before the day on which M. Bernardon would have this brief conversation with Prisoner number 2,224 in the Toulon penal colony, the Morénas family, consisting of a widow and her two sons, Pierre, at that time twenty-five years old, and Jean, five years his junior, lived happily together in the village of Sainte-Marie-des-Maures.

Both young men practised the trade of carpenter and there was no shortage of employment for them, either within their own village community or in the surrounding villages. Both being equally skilled, their services were equally in demand.

What was unequal, however, was the level of public esteem enjoyed by each, and it must be admitted that this difference in regard was justified. While the younger son, very hard-working in his dedication to his craft, and passionately adoring in his devotion to this beloved mother, might have served as a model to all sons, the older was regularly prone to misconduct and anti-social behaviour. Violent and hot-headed, he would often, after a few drinks, become the main protagonist in arguments or even brawls, and his tongue would let him down badly, even more so than his acts. Indeed, his ill-advised and thoughtless words flowed freely. He would curse his narrow, confined existence in this little corner of the mountains and proclaim his desire to set off to pastures new, to make his fortune, which, he had no doubt, would be quickly acquired. The fact is that this sort of attitude is all it takes to arouse distrust within the tradition-loving souls of local country people. Nevertheless, no serious grievance could really be levelled at this young man, which is why people were usually content to think of him as a bit of a hot-headed dare-devil, just as capable of good deeds as of wrong-doing, depending on the vagaries of what life brought his way—though they continued to be more unequivocal in having an unreservedly favourable opinion of his younger brother.

The Morénas family was therefore a happy one, in spite of these slight storm-clouds on the horizon. Their happiness stemmed from their perfect unity. No serious criticism could, all things considered, be levelled at either of these two young men as sons; and as brothers, they loved each other with all their heart, so that anybody who tried to attack one of them would have had two adversaries to contend with.

The first misfortune which was to strike the Morénas family was the sudden disappearance of the older son. The very day on which he reached his twenty-fifth birthday, he left as usual to go to work, which, that day, necessitated his travelling to a neighbouring village. That evening, his mother and brother waited in vain for his return: Pierre Morénas did not come back.

What had become of him? Had he been overwhelmed or killed in one of his usual bouts of fisticuffs? Had he been the victim of an accident or a crime? Had he simply decided to run away? None of these questions were ever to be answered.

His mother's despair was heart-rending. In time, the passage of months and years being able to heal all wounds, life began to resume, little by little, its peaceful, routine course. Gradually, helped in no small measure by the loving support of her second son, Madame Morénas came to experience a sense of resignation—albeit tinged by melancholy—an acceptance which is the only joy allowed to hearts which have been wounded by adversity.

Five years went by in this manner, five years throughout which the loving devotion of the dedicated son that was Jean Morénas was constant, never failing for one single second. It was at the end of these five years, just as Jean himself reached, in his turn, the age of twenty-five, that a second and even more terrible misfortune came to crush this family which had already been so cruelly tested by fate.

At some short distance from the small house in which she lived, the widow's own brother, Alexandre Tisserand, ran the village's only inn. There lived with Uncle Sandy—as Jean was in the habit of calling him—his goddaughter, Marie. A long time previously, he had taken her in, following the death of the little girl's parents. Having come to live at the inn, she never left it. Helping her benefactor and godfather in the running of the humble hostelry, she had lived and grown up there, moving successively through the stages of childhood and teenage years. At the time when Jean Morénas reached his twenty-fifth birthday, she herself was eighteen years old, and the little girl of before had now become a young woman, as sweet and mild-mannered as she was pretty.

She and Jean had grown up together, enjoying each other's company as they played their childhood games, and the old inn had, on numerous occasions, resounded to the joyful sounds of their childish frolics. Then, by degrees, their sources of playful amusement had altered in nature, at the same time as a gradual change began to take place, at least within Jean's heart, to the innocent childhood friendship of days gone by.

The day thus arrived when Jean came to love as a fiancée the girl whom he had, up to then, regarded as a much-loved sister. His love for her was in keeping with his honourable, gentlemanly nature, in the same way that he loved his mother, with the same self-effacing devotion, the same zeal, and with the same whole-hearted dedication of his entire being.

He kept his silence, however, and said nothing of his intentions to this young woman whom he hoped to one day make his wife. The fact of the matter was, as he understood only too well, that the platonic tenderness felt for him by the young woman had not developed in the same way as had his own feelings for her. While his own fraternal devotion to her had been gradually transformed into love, Marie's heart remained the same as always. She would look at her childhood companion with the same innocent serenity in her pure blue eyes, which continued to be unclouded by any new or confusing emotions.

Conscious of this discrepancy in their respective feelings for each other, Jean thus kept his counsel and nurtured his secret romantic hopes hidden deep within his heart, much to the sadness of Uncle Sandy, who held his nephew in the greatest of esteem and would thus have been more than happy to entrust to him both his goddaughter and the few coppers he had built up over forty years of persistent hard work. And yet, for all that, the good uncle had not given up hope. Things could still work out for the best: Marie was still very young. With the benefit of increasing maturity, she might well come to recognise the fine qualities of Jean Morénas who, thus emboldened, would make his marriage proposal, which would then be favorably received.

Things were at this point, when a sudden and unexpected tragedy shattered the peace of the little village of Sainte-Marie-des-Maures. One morning, Uncle Sandy was found dead, strangled, in front of his bar counter, the cash-drawer of which had been emptied down to the very last farthing. Who was responsible for this heinous, murderous crime? The police might have investigated in vain for quite some time, if the dead man himself had not gone to the trouble of indicating the identity of his killer: in the clenched fist of the corpse was found, in fact, a crumpled piece of paper on which, just before breathing his last, Alexander Tisserand had managed to write the following words: "It's my nephew who…." He had not had the strength to write any more than this, and death had stayed his hand in the middle of the accusing sentence.

Yet for all that, these words proved more than sufficient. Alexandre Tisserand had only one nephew: there could be no possible doubt as to the culprit.

The crime was reconstructed without difficulty. The previous evening, there had been nobody at the inn. The murderer had therefore arrived from somewhere outside the premises, and must have been somebody well-known to the victim, since Alexander Tisserand, usually of a very wary disposition, had opened the door to him without raising any difficulties. It was equally certain that the crime had been committed early in the evening, as the victim was still fully clothed. It could be deduced from the unfinished accounts remaining on the counter-top, that he had been engaged in checking his takings and writing up his accounts at the moment when the visitor had appeared. When he went to open the door to let him in, he had automatically brought with him the pencil he had been using, and which he would later use in order to identify his killer.

No sooner had he gained entry than the latter had seized his victim by the neck and knocked him down. The entire tragedy must have played out within a couple of minutes. There were, indeed, no signs of a struggle, and Marie, who had been in her bedroom—admittedly quite a distance from the bar—had not heard any sound of disturbance.

Reckoning the innkeeper to be dead, the murderous assailant had emptied the cash-drawer, and had thoroughly rummaged throughout the sleeping quarters, as was evident from the overturned bed and the cupboards which had been knocked down. Finally, having pocketed his ill-gotten spoils, the killer had quickly taken flight, leaving no traces of evidence which might be likely to incriminate him.

Or so he had presumed—but the wretched man had not bargained for the fact that "justice will out": the man whom he believed dead was, in fact, still alive, and for a couple of minutes had regained consciousness. He had just about found the strength to write out those four words which were to quickly lead the investigation to follow a definite line of enquiry, though the words were tragically cut short by a final, fatal spasm as he lay in the throes of death.

The reaction in the village was one of stupefied disbelief. Jean Morénas, that good workman and devoted son—a murderer! And yet there could be no option but to accept the overwhelming, damning evidence, and the dead man's accusation was too categorical to allow room for any doubt. This was, at least, the opinion of the legal system. Despite his protestations of innocence, Jean Morénas was arrested, tried and sentenced to twenty years of hard labor.

This horrifying tragedy was the culmination of his poor mother's misfortunes. From that day onwards, her health began to decline very quickly. Less than a year later, she followed her murdered brother to the grave.

A merciless fate had caused her to die prematurely. Her death came at the very moment when, after so much suffering, a cause for joy was finally about to come her way. The last sod of earth had hardly been thrown onto her coffin, when who should reappear in the area but none other than her older son Pierre.

Where had he come from? What had he been doing throughout these six years that he had been away? What regions had he travelled through? In what circumstances was he now returning to his native village? But Pierre deigned to offer no explanations on this score, and despite the level of local curiosity, people eventually grew weary of speculating to each other about his circumstances.

Moreover, even if he hadn't made his fortune, in the strict sense of the term, it certainly seemed that at least he hadn't come back penniless; indeed, he now only practised his former trade of carpenter on a sporadic basis, and for the next two years, he practically lived the life of a gentleman of independent means at Sainte-Marie-des-Maures, only very seldom leaving the village to go to Marseilles, where, he would explain, he had business dealings to transact.

Throughout these two years, he spent most of his time, not in the house he had inherited from his late mother, but in Uncle Sandy's inn, which had now come into Marie's ownership; since the tragic death of her godfather, Marie was now running the hostelry with the help of a manservant.

Just as one might easily imagine, a love affair gradually blossomed between the two young people. That romantic goal which had not been achieved by the gentle zeal of Jean, was reached through the bluster and somewhat rough-edged character of Pierre. To the increasing romantic attachment which the latter felt for her, Marie responded with comparable love. And so, two years after the death of the widow Morénas, three years after the death of Uncle Sandy and the sentencing of his killer, the wedding of these two young people took place.

Seven years went by, during which time three children were born to them, the youngest child arriving hardly six months prior to the day on which our story begins. By this time, Marie had experienced seven years of wedded bliss as a happy wife and mother. Yet she would have been less happy had she been able to read into the secret soul of her husband, if she had known of the vagrant life which, over a period of six years—graduating from petty theft to the stealing of larger amounts, from there to fraud, and onwards to full-blown robbery—had been led by this man to whom her life was now joined; and she would have been especially unhappy had she known the part her husband had played in the murder of her godfather.

Alexandre Tisserand had told the truth when his note had incriminated his nephew, but how regrettable it is that, in the throes of death which had confused his brain and weakened his hand, as he struggled to write, he had been thwarted from being more specific! It was indeed his nephew who was responsible for this heinous crime, but the nephew in question was not Jean—it was Pierre Morénas.

Having completely run out of means of subsistence, reduced to the most abject state of poverty, Pierre had returned to Sainte-Marie-des-Maures after nightfall, having firmly resolved to help himself to his uncle's nest-egg. But the resistance put up by the victim had turned the thief into a murderer.

Having knocked the innkeeper out, he had proceeded to completely loot the premises before taking flight, vanishing into the darkness. He had thus known nothing of his uncle's death—imagining him to have been merely unconscious—nor of the arrest and conviction of his brother. It was thus in a completely untroubled state of mind that, a year after his crime, and seeing his ill-gotten gains frittering away, he returned to his native soil, confident in the expectation that his crime would be forgiven without difficulty, as so much time had passed. It was only then that he learned of the death of his uncle and of his mother, and of his brother's conviction for murder.

At first he was devastated. The tragic circumstances of his younger brother—to whom he had been linked by such true, deep affection for twenty years—became, for Pierre, a source of bitter remorse. Yet what could he do now, to rectify the situation, other than revealing the truth, and, in the process, giving himself up and taking the place of the wrongfully convicted man in the penal colony?

Under the influence of passing time, sorrow and remorse began to fade; love did the rest.

But his remorse returned to haunt him once married life had become well and truly established upon its peaceful course. With each passing day, the memory of the innocent convict imposed itself every more forcefully on the mind and conscience of the unpunished guilty party. Reminiscences of their childhood years became unceasingly stronger in his memory, and the day eventually came when Pierre Morénas began to dream of how he might go about rescuing his brother from the ball and chain to which he himself had shackled him. After all, he was no longer the penniless, destitute rogue who had left Sainte-Marie-des-Maures in order to seek his unattainable fortune in the wide world. The former beggar was now a property owner, the wealthiest man in his village, and was thus not short of a penny or two. Could this money not now be used in order to expunge his remorse?

Chapter V

Jean Morénas continued to watch M. Bernardon as he walked away, following him with his eyes until he was out of sight. He had difficulty in understanding what was happening to him. How did this stranger come to be so intimately acquainted with the diverse circumstances of his personal life?

That was certainly an insoluble conundrum. However, whether he understood it or not, it was essential, whatever the case may be, to accept the offer which had now been made to him. He therefore resolved to prepare for escape.

Before doing anything else, however, he considered it necessary to inform his companion-in-chains of the escape bid he was contemplating. There was no avoiding this disclosure, as the chain which linked them together could not be broken by one, without the other becoming immediately aware of it; although Romain would perhaps then wish to also benefit from this opportunity to escape, which would reduce its prospects of success.

As the elderly convict had only eighteen months remaining to serve in chains, Jean strove to convince him that it was not worthwhile risking an increased sentence with such little time remaining. But Romain, who could ultimately sense the lure of money at the end of all this, would not listen to reason, and stubbornly refused to have any hand, act or part in co-operating with the schemes of his comrade in the chain gang. However, as soon as the latter began to talk about a thousand francs payable up front, and a similar amount which the old man might well expect upon his release from the penal colony, Romain began to no longer turn a deaf ear, and rather, to come around to his chain gang-mate's way of thinking.

Once this matter had been settled, it remained for Jean to decide on the means of making good his escape. The essential matter was to leave the port without being spotted, and thus to avoid being seen by the sentries or the prison guards. As soon as he had reached the open countryside, and before the *gendarmerie* had been notified of his escape, it would be an easy matter to feign a different identity among the local country people, and as for those among them who might be rendered more perceptive by the prospect of a reward from the police, they would surely not resist the lure of a greater sum of money from the escapee himself.

Jean Morénas resolved to break out under cover of darkness. Even though he was a fixed-term prisoner, he was not incarcerated in one of the old ships which had been converted into a floating prison: he was one of the exceptions who happened to be imprisoned in one of the penal colonies on dry land. To exit from these would have been difficult; it was therefore important not to go back in there in the evening after his day's labors. As the harbour was pretty much deserted at evening time, it would probably not be impossible for him to swim across it. Indeed, he could not realistically aspire to leaving the shipyard through any route other than by sea. As soon as he had regained dry land, it would be up to his newfound protector to come to his assistance.

Thus led by his reflections to trust in the unknown, he resolved to await the further guidance of his mysterious patron, and to see whether the promises made to Romain would indeed be kept. Time seemed to go by too slowly as he waited impatiently to see how events would continue to unfold.

It was not until two days later that his mysterious friend reappeared.

"Well?" asked M. Bernardon.

"Everything's been agreed on and arranged, Sir, and since you wish to be of service to me, I can assure you that everything will go according to plan."

"What do you need?"

"I've promised two thousand francs to my comrade in chains, including one thousand of that when he gets out of prison..."

"He shall have it. What else?"

"And a thousand francs up front."

"Here they are," said M. Bernardon, handing over the requested sum, which the old convict immediately caused to seemingly vanish into thin air.

The stranger from Marseilles continued: "Here is some gold, and one of the best-toughened files you can get hold of. Will that be enough for you to get the better of those chains, do you think?"

"Yes, sir. Where shall I see you again?"

"At Cape Brun. You will find me on the shore, at the far end of the cove known as Port Mejean. Do you know it?"

"Yes. You can count on me."

"When are you leaving here?"

"Tonight—I'm going to swim for it."

"Are you a strong swimmer?"

"As strong as they come—first-class."

"That's good—all is in our favour then. So, I shall see you later tonight."

"See you later tonight!"

M. Bernardon then took his leave of the two convicts, who now returned to their labors. Without taking any further notice of the pair, the gentleman from Marseille continued his lengthy walk round the port, occasionally questioning and conversing with different people, before finally leaving the shipyard, without at all arousing suspicion or coming to anybody's notice.

Chapter VI

Jean Morénas studiously applied himself to appearing to be the calmest prisoner imaginable. Despite his efforts, however, an attentive observer would have been struck by his unaccustomed degree of restlessness. The love of freedom made his heart beat strongly, and the strength of his entire willpower was simply incapable of overcoming his fevered impatience. How far away it seemed now, that superficial stoical acceptance of his lot, with which, for the past ten years, he had emotionally armor-plated himself against despair!

In order to conceal his absence for several minutes, that evening, from among the returned prisoners, he had come up with the idea of replacing himself with one of his fellow prisoners, who would stand beside his companion-in-chains. One of the convicts known as the *chaussettes* or *old rags*—so-called because of the light ring which the galley prisoners belonging to this category wear round their leg—who had only a few days left in the penal colony, and had therefore been unlinked from his chains, came round to Jean's way of thinking in exchange for three gold coins, and agreed to fasten the latter's chain to his own foot for several minutes, as soon as the irons had been severed.

A little after seven o'clock that evening, Jean took advantage of a break from the day's labors in order to saw through his irons. Thanks to the perfect quality of the file, and despite his shackles being of a particularly high calibre of iron, he managed to quickly discharge this task. And at the moment when the convicts were going back into their prison quarters—the *chaussette* prisoner having by this time taken his place—Jean hid by huddling up behind a stacked-up pile of timber.

Not far from where he now stood, there was an enormous boiler which was intended for a ship currently under construction. This huge tank had been placed upon its base, and the opening in the furnaces offered the fugitive an impenetrable refuge. Benefiting from an opportune moment, the escaped prisoner slipped noiselessly into this hiding place, taking with him the end-piece of a wooden beam which he hastily hollowed out to from a makeshift hat which he then pierced with holes. Next, he watched and waited, eyes and ears peeled, nerves stretched tense, almost to breaking point.

Night began to fall. The cloud-laden sky thickened the darkness and was thus favourable to Jean Morénas. At the other side of the harbour, the Saint-Madrier peninsula was being swallowed up into invisibility by the descending darkness.

Once the dockyard was deserted, Jean exited from his hiding place, and creeping cautiously along, made his way towards the careening docks.[1] A few warrant officers wandered round here and there. At times, Jean would come to a dead halt and flatten himself against the ground. Fortunately, he had succeeded in breaking his irons, thus allowing him to move about noiselessly.

He finally reached the water's edge, on a quay of the New Port, not far from the opening which provided access into the harbour. With his makeshift hat in hand, he slid down a rope and disappeared beneath the waves.

When he came back up to the surface, he quickly covered himself with this bizarre headdress and thus became invisible to all searching eyes. The holes which he had previously cut into the wooden cap allowed him to see where he was going. This cap might have been supposed to be a mooring buoy floating along.

Suddenly, the roar of cannon fire rang out.

"It's the closing of the port," thought Jean Morénas.

There was a second, then a third, burst of fire.

There could be no mistaking what this sound meant; it was the alarm cannon. Jean realised that his escape had been discovered.

Carefully avoiding the approaching ships and the chains of anchors, he made his way forward through the waters of the small harbour, towards the Millau powder magazine. The sea was a little

---

1. In nautical terminology, careening is a process whereby vessels are keeled over onto one side for repair and/or cleaning.

rough, but the powerful swimmer felt sufficiently strong to vanquish its resistance. His clothes, hindering his progress, had been cast off into the water as he went along, and all he had kept was the purse of gold coins tied round his chest.

He reached the middle of the small harbour without meeting any obstacles.

There, leaning against one of those iron mooring buoys which are popularly known as *dead bodies*, he carefully removed the makeshift hat which protected him, and got his breath back.[2]

"Phew!" he said to himself, "this outing so far is only a Sunday afternoon stroll compared to what I've still got to do. Once I'm out in the open sea, I won't have to worry about running into anybody, but I'll first of all have to get past the harbour bottleneck, where lots of ships sail from the Great Tower to the Needlepoint Fort. It'll be the luck of the devil if I manage to escape their notice… In the meantime, let me get my bearings, and not do anything stupid to end up throwing myself into the lion's jaws!"

Using the Lagoubran powder magazine and the Fort of Saint-Louis as reference points, Jean calculated his exact position, and then resumed swimming.

With his head sheltered underneath his makeshift headgear, he swam cautiously. As the sound of the freshening wind might prevent him from hearing other, more dangerous, noises, he remained on his guard and, however important it might have been for him to get clear of the small harbour, he progressed with deliberate slowness, so as the so-called mooring buoy which covered him would not be conferred with an unlikely, suspicious degree of speed.

Half an hour went by. According to his calculations, he must be near to the channel, when, to his left, he thought he could hear the sound of oars. He stopped, listening carefully.

"Hey!," somebody shouted from a small open boat, "What's the latest?"

"Nothing new to report," somebody else replied from another boat, this time to the fugitive's right.

"We'll never be able to catch him!"

"But is it definite that he's escaped by sea?"

---

2. Dead bodies: *Corps morts* is the term used by Verne, a slang term for mooring buoys.

Some adjutants were still here and there.

"Nothing surer! His clothes have been fished up."

"It's so dark that he could end up bringing us all the way to India!"

"Go to it, lads! Row steadily!"

The boats sailed away from each other. As soon as they were far enough away from him, Jean chanced a few more vigorous strokes and quickly progressed towards the harbour bottleneck.

According as he got nearer to it, the shouts became more and more frequent all around him, as the boats which criss-crossed the harbour were, of necessity, concentrating their search and surveillance around this point. Without allowing himself be intimidated by the sheer number of his adversaries, Jean continued to swim.

A few warrant officers wandered about here and there, but with all the strength he could summon, Jean kept swimming onwards. He had decided to himself that he would sooner drown than be recaptured, and that these hunters would not take him alive.

It was not long before the shapes of the Great Tower and the Needlepoint Fort were outlined before his eyes.

Torch lights streaked across the sea wall and along the shore; the *gendarmerie* squads had already been put into operation and were in action. The fugitive slowed his pace and allowed himself to be carried along by the waves and the west wind, which were driving him onwards and outwards towards the open sea.

The waves were suddenly illuminated by the light of a torch, and Jean spotted four boats which had, by now, encircled him. He no longer moved a muscle, as the slightest movement could prove to be his downfall.

"Hey! What news from your boat?" a voice called out from one of the small vessels.

"Not a thing!"

"Let's keep going!"

Jean allowed himself to breathe again. The boats were about to move away, and it was about time. They were less than ten fathoms away, and their closeness forced him to swim at a right angle to them.[3]

"Hold on a minute! What's that over there?" shouted one of the sailors.

"What?" came the reply.

"That floating black spot."

---

3.   A nautical fathom is about six feet.

"It's nothing. A mooring buoy afloat."

"Well, get hold of it!"

Jean held himself at the ready to dive beneath the waves, but then, the whistle of a petty officer was heard.[4]

"Sail on, lads! We have better things to be doing than fishing up the end of a wooden beam… Everyone keep moving forward…"

The oars loudly smote the waves. The misfortunate escapee took heart; his ruse had not been uncovered. With renewed hope came increased strength, and he set off once again towards the Needlepoint Fort, whose massive bulk now rose up before him.

Suddenly, he found himself plunged into the deepest darkness. A hazy object blocked his view of the Fort. It was one of the boats, which, having been launched at full speed, now struck him; following the collision, one of the sailors leaned over the side of the boat.

"It's a mooring buoy," he said, reaching the same conclusion as his comrade had previously done.

The small boat resumed its onward progression. But by an unfortunate turn of events, one of the oars struck the fake mooring buoy and knocked it over. Before the escaped prisoner could even think about concealing himself from view, his shaved head had revealed itself above the water.

"We've got him" cried the sailors. "Go to it, lads!"

Jean plunged himself into the waves, and as whistles sounded out in every direction, summoning the boats which were scattered about, he swam just below the surface in the direction of Lazaret strand. By doing this he was moving farther away from the appointed meeting place, as this strand is to the right of the entrance to the large harbour, whereas Cape Brun jutted out to Jean's left; but he was hoping to put his foes off the scent, by making for the area which was least favourable to his escape bid.

But for all that, he would still have to reach the place which had been indicated by the stranger from Marseilles. Thus, having swum a few strokes in the opposite direction, Jean Morénas returned to his original route. All around him, boats cut across each other. He was

---

4. The original uses the term "quartier-maître" which can be translated by such terms as "leading seaman" or "petty officer third class," as close target culture equivalents, e.g. the latter term is a closely equivalent U.S. Navy rank, according to the *Collins Robert French Dictionary* (Eighth Edition, 2006).

constantly having to dive underwater to avoid being seen. But in the end, his skilful tactics outwitted his pursuers, and he succeeded in putting a distance between himself and his hunters as he swam in the right direction.

But was it too late? Wearied by this protracted struggle against men and against the elements, Jean could feel himself getting weaker. His strength was diminishing. Several times, his eyes closed, and his brain was filled with dizzying, swirling sensations; a few times, his hands became slack, and his feet, feeling heavier and heavier, would start to sink into the watery depths…

By what miracle did he reach dry land? He himself would have been unable to say. Nonetheless, reach it he did. Suddenly, he felt that he was on *terra firma*. He stood up, took a few teetering steps, lurched and keeled over into a dead faint, but beyond the reach of the waves.

When he came to, a man was leaning over him, applying, to his tightly-set lips, the neck of a wineskin bottle, from which a few drops of brandy were being gently poured.

Chapter VII

The countryside situated to the east of Toulon, teeming as it is with woods and mountains, criss-crossed by ravines and watercourses, presented the fugitive with numerous opportunities for salvation. Now that he had reached dry land, he had a realistic hope of completely regaining his freedom. Feeling reassured on this score, Jean Morénas now felt a resurgence of the curiosity which his generous protector awoke within him. He could not guess at his motivations. Was it because this stranger from Marseilles was in need of an enterprising, robust fellow, prepared for anything and completely fearless, that he had gone and chosen him at the penal colony? If that was the case, M. Bernardon would be barking up the wrong tree, as Jean Morénas had firmly resolved to reject any dubious propositions.

"Are you feeling better?" asked M. Bernardon, having allowed the fugitive time to recover. "Are you strong enough to walk?"

"Yes," replied Jean, as he stood up.

"In that case, put on this local countryman's clothing which I've brought for you. Then we'll be on our way! We don't have a minute to lose."

It was eleven o'clock at night when the two men set off into the countryside, avoiding the more frequently-travelled roads, hurling themselves down into ditches and copses whenever the sound of footsteps or of a cart rang out in the midst of the silence. Although the fugitive's disguise rendered him unrecognizable, they were very wary of attracting undue notice, as the Provençal costume which Jean had put on could have a somewhat "borrowed" look.

Other than the squads of gendarmes, which are marshalled and go into action the moment the first roar of the alarm cannon is heard, Jean Morénas had reason to dread any passer-by. A concern for their safety, and also the lure of the State reward for the recapture of an escaped convict, tends to increase the sharpness of the country folk's watchful eyes, the speed of their legs and the strength of their arms. The fact is that any fugitive runs a strong risk of being recognized, either because, accustomed to the weight of the irons, he drags his leg a little, or because some tell-tale look of distress appears on his face.

Having walked for three solid hours, the two men stopped on a signal from M. Bernardon. The latter now took, from a pouch-shaped bag which he carried over his shoulder, some provisions, which were greedily devoured from underneath the shelter of a thick hedge. [1]

"Get some sleep now," said the stranger from Marseille, once this quick meal had been eaten. "You've got a long way to go, so you must conserve your energy."

Jean didn't need to be asked twice, and, stretching himself out on the ground, he fell like a dead weight into a profound slumber.

Morning had broken when M. Bernardon woke him. Both men immediately set off again on foot. They were now no longer seeking to slip quickly across the fields. From now on, the strategy to be adopted involved not concealing themselves from view, while nonetheless being seen as little as possible; not avoiding being looked at, though not subjecting themselves to closer scrutiny, and conspicuously following the main roads.

M. Bernardon and Jean Morénas had been walking for a long time when the latter thought he heard the trot of several horses.

He climbed up onto an embankment in order to have a clear view of the road, but a bend in the highway prevented him from seeing anything. However, he could not have been mistaken. Lying down, his ear close to the ground, he strove to recognize the sound which had struck him.

Before he could get back on his feet, M. Bernardon had thrown himself on top of him, pinning him to the ground. In the blink of an eye, Jean found himself securely bound and gagged.

---

1. A pouch-shaped bag: The French term used is "un bissac," literally "a double bag"; this French word dates from the fifteenth century and is now archaic and has fallen into disuse. It describes a sort of bag carried by shepherds and pilgrims in previous centuries; a long bag, open in the middle, with a pocket at each end.

A man leaned over him.

At this same moment, two police officers on horseback came out onto the open road. They came level with M. Bernardon, who continued to maintain a tight, firm grip on his flabbergasted prisoner. One of them now questioned the gentleman from Marseilles:

"Now then, my good man, what's the meaning of all this?"

"This is an escaped convict, officer; an escaped convict whom I've just managed to recapture," replied M. Bernardon.

"Oh! Indeed!" said the policeman. "You mean, the fellow from last night?"

"It could well be. In any case, whether it's him or someone else, I've got him."

"You've earned yourself a generous reward, my friend!"

"That's not to be sneezed at, not to mention the fact that his clothes are not prison-standard. I'll get those into the bargain."

"Do you need our help?" asked one of the policemen.

"My goodness, no! He's solidly anchored to me, I'll be well able to bring him off on my own."

"That's for the best," the policeman replied. "Good bye, and good luck!"

The police officers went on their way. When they had disappeared from view, M. Bernardon stopped in a copse at the edge of the roadway. In an instant, the ropes binding Jean Morénas had fallen away.

"You are free," his companion told him, indicating a westerly direction to him. "Make your way along this road, heading west. With endurance, you can be in Marseilles by tonight. Go to the old port and look for the *Mary-Magdalene*, a three-master laden with cargo, bound for Valparaiso in Chile.[2] The captain has been notified to expect you and will take you on board. Your name is Jacques Reynaud; here are identity papers bearing that name. You've got some gold in your pocket. Try to start a new life; God be with you."

Before Jean Morénas could respond, M. Bernardon had vanished into the trees. The fugitive stood alone on the roadside.

2. Could there be some symbolic significance in the choice of the name of the New Testament's redeemed and forgiven sinner, Mary Magdalene, for the ship, given that the primary themes of *Morénas* include sin, the search for redemption, and the granting of forgiveness?

Chapter VIII

Jean Morénas stood motionless for quite some time, stupefied at this outcome to his incredible adventure. Why was his protector suddenly abandoning him, after helping him to escape? Above all, why had this stranger taken an interest in the fate of a prisoner who didn't seem to have any reason to come to his particular attention? What was the stranger's name, even? Jean realised that he hadn't even thought of asking the name of his savior.

Though there was no longer any means of redressing this lapse on his part, it was, all in all, of little importance. The crucial matter was that he was no longer dragging the irons which had bruised him to the very bone for so long. Everything else would be explained later; or perhaps never. One thing he could be sure of, in any event, was that he was alone on the edge of a deserted road, with gold in his pocket, equipped with official identity documentation, and filling his lungs with the heady air of freedom.

Jean Morénas set off again on foot. He had been told to make his way to Marseilles. It was, therefore, towards Marseilles that he now directed his footsteps, without even giving the matter any thought, only to come to a halt after just a few steps.

Marseilles, the *Mary Magdalene*, Valparaiso in Chili, starting a new life; what a load of stuff and nonsense! Was it in order to "start a new life" in distant lands that he had yearned so strongly for freedom? No, no! Throughout his long captivity, he had dreamed of one place only: Sainte-Marie-des-Maures, and of only one being in the whole

Jean prowled through the empty and silent streets.

world: Marguerite.[1] It was his homesickness for his native village, and memories of Marguerite, that had made his imprisonment so cruel, his chains so heavy. And now, he was going to leave without even trying to see them again? Come on! At that rate of going, he may as well return and submit to the cudgel of the prison guards!

No: to see his village once again, to kneel down at his mother's grave, and above all, see Marguerite once more, that is what he must do at all costs. When he found himself once more in the presence of the young woman, he would be able to summon the courage which he had lacked in the past. He would explain himself, he would talk to her, he would prove his innocence. Marguerite was no longer a child; maybe now, she would reciprocate his love for her. If that was the case, he would be able to persuade her to go with him. What a blissfully happy future now lay in store for him! If, on the other hand, she did not feel the same way about him as he did about her, then whatever was meant to be, would be, and would no longer have any importance whatsoever.

Jean, leaving the main road, took the first dirt road which he came across, travelling in a northerly direction. But soon, he stopped again, realising once more—through his very desire to succeed in his goal—that caution was the wisest option. He was only too familiar with the countryside that he was crossing, and over which he had so often travelled in his childhood, not to be aware that the destination he wished to reach was not all that distant from him. He could be in Sainte-Marie-des-Maures within two hours, but it was important not to enter the village until it was pitch dark, for fear of being arrested the moment he set foot in the place.

Jean thus lingered a while in the countryside, and did not set off again in earnest until twilight, and following a long sleep and a restorative meal in an open-air eating house.[2]

Nine o'clock was ringing, and the darkness was deep, when he reached the houses of Sainte-Marie-des-Maures. He slipped quietly through the deserted, noiseless laneways, without being seen by anyone, until he came to Uncle Sandy's inn.

---

1. The name of Jean's unrequited love is here, inexplicably, changed from "Marie" to "Marguerite"; this appears to be an error on the author's part.

2. The French term is *une guingette*, a culture-specific reference to typically French open-air cafés with music and dancing.

How could he gain access to the inn? Through the door? Certainly not. Did he have any idea who might be inside the main room, and whether, behind the door, he might not come up against some enemy or other? What was more, did the inn still belong to Marguerite? Why, after so many years, might it not have passed into new hands?

Very fortunately, he had a better and safer way of getting into the place than through the door.

It is not rare for traditional Provencal houses to have secret exits, allowing their dwellers to come and go incognito. These "contraptions," which vary in the level of ingenuity with which they have been devised, were probably conceived during the religious wars which had set these regions aflame and caused them to flow with blood. Nothing could be more natural than the fact that the people living during these troubled times should have sought some means of escaping, where necessary, from their enemies.

This secret passageway in Uncle Sandy's inn, a secret which had quite certainly remained unknown to the owner, had been discovered by Jean and Marguerite, by chance, in the course of one of their childhood games, and, proud of being the only ones to be "in on" this secret, they had taken care not to reveal its existence to anybody at all. Having grown to adulthood, they had, in turn, forgotten all about it, so that Jean could now quite legitimately hope to find the mechanism intact, at the very moment that he needed to make use of it.

The secret lay in the movableness of the back of the fireplace within the main room of the inn. As is the case in many rural buildings, this fireplace was huge, and sufficiently wide and deep—the tiny hearth taking up only the centre—to hide several people within its shelter. The back of the fireplace consisted of two enormous cast-iron parallel firebacks, a few decimetres apart from each other.[3] These two slabs were moveable and could swivel round lightly at the push of a handle operated in the right way. It was therefore possible for anybody who was privy to the secret—the existence of which, moreover, was not in any way likely to be suspected by anyone—to gain access into the space which had been worked between the two slabs; then, having shut the slab which had yielded a right of way to him or her, it was possible to half-open the other one and thus move from inside the house to the outside, or vice versa.

---

3.   A fireback is an ornamental (though not uniquely so, in this case) iron slab against the back wall of a hearth.

Jean walked round the house, and, moving his hand over the surface of the wall, he found, without too much trouble, the outside slab. A few minutes's investigation led him to recognize the handle, which he turned in the necessary manner. Quite clearly, nothing had been changed. The handle yielded to his efforts, and the iron slab, with a dull rumbling sound, was pushed back under the pressure.

Jean let himself in through this gap, then, having once more closed the slab, paused to recover his breath.

He needed to act with ever-increasing caution. A ray of light filtered into his hiding place, through the edge of the inside fireback, and the sound of voices came from the main room. They had not yet gone to sleep in the inn. Before revealing his presence, he needed to find out who he could expect to be dealing with.

Unfortunately, despite his best efforts in casting his eyes all round the fireback, it was impossible for him to see anything. Weary from his efforts, he resolved to open the slab half-way, though this was a high-risk strategy…

At this very moment, the sound of a loud din rose up within the main room. It was, at first, a piercing cry, a cry for help, the cry of somebody in the throes of death, immediately followed by a sort of groan; then there were gasps for breath, which sounded like the puffs of a forge, akin to the panting of two people struggling in combat with each other, accompanied by the crash of an overturned piece of furniture.

After a brief moment of hesitation, Jean brought his weight to bear on the handle. The iron slab slid round, revealing, in its entirety, the common room of the inn.

But just after he had burst forward into the main room, Jean retreated to the shelter of the shadows filling the fireplace, and of the smoke rising from a few twigs remaining in the grate, terrified by the scene which he found unfolding before his eyes.

Chapter IX

At the heavy table which occupied the centre of the room, a man was sitting, whom another man, standing behind him, was strangling, with a supreme effort of his entire being. It was the former who, having felt himself grasped round the neck, had first cried out, then groaned; but it was from the chest of the latter that there now escaped this husky breathing, like that of an athlete putting all his strength into overcoming an opponent. In the struggle, a chair had fallen over.

In front of the seated man, an ink bottle and some writing paper indicated that he had been in the process of writing when his enemy had sprung unexpectedly upon him. Within reach of his hand, on the table, there was a half-open bag from which could be seen the papers with which it was full.

The scene had by now lasted hardly a minute, but was already coming to an end. The seated man had already stopped struggling, and all that could now be heard was the panting of his murderer. In any case, the incident could not possibly have gone on any longer; the victim's cries had been heard. People were bustling about outside. From within a bedroom on the first floor of the inn, led to by a wooden gallery which was reached by a stairwell mounting from the main room, Jean heard two bare feet landing heavily on the tiled floor. Upstairs, somebody had just got out of bed. In another moment, a door would open and a witness would arrive onto the scene.

The murderer realised the danger he was in. His hands loosened their stranglehold and—while the victim's head flopped heavily and insensibly onto the table—plunged into the bag, from which they withdrew a tightly-gripped wad of banknotes. The man then leapt backwards and disappeared through a small doorway under the stairs, leading to the cellar.

His face thus became visible, for a second, in the full glare of light. Jean Morénas, frantic with terror, thrown into turmoil, did not need any longer than this to recognize him.

This man was none other than the stranger who had caused the chains of the innocent convict to fall away; who had given him gold; had protected him, and guided him through the countryside until they had been only a few kilometres from Sainte-Marie-des-Maures. In vain had he dispensed with the fake beard and wig with which

"Criminal!" she shouted.

he had sought to alter his facial features; there remained his eyes, forehead, nose, mouth and build, and there was no way Jean could be mistaken.

But the removal of the disguise of the false beard and of the wig had another, altogether more surprising and disturbing consequence. In this man, to whom had thus been restored his true appearance; in this man who had just revealed himself to be both his savior and a murderer, Jean was stupefied to recognize his brother, Pierre, who had long ago vanished and whom he had not seen in fifteen years!

For what mysterious reasons were his brother and his savior one and the same person? Through what combination of circumstances did Pierre Morénas happen to be, that day, in Uncle Sandy's inn of all places? In what capacity was he there? Why had he chosen this place as the scene of his crime?

These questions rushed tumultuously through Jean's mind. The facts, in response, spoke for themselves.

Hardly had the killer vanished than a door was opened on the first floor.

On the wooden gallery, there now appeared a young woman, up against whom there squeezed two pyjama-clad children, and who was holding a third child, a toddler, in her arms. Jean recognized Marguerite! Marguerite, with children! Her own children, by all accounts! So, she had renounced and forgotten the innocent man who, far from her, loitered and shrivelled away in the prison colony?[1] The unfortunate man instantly understood how futile his hopes had been.

"Pierre!… my Pierre!" the young woman called out, in a voice which trembled with anguish.

She suddenly became aware of the man who had fallen forward, senseless, onto the table. "Oh my God," she murmured, hurriedly descending the stairs, her toddler in her arms, the two other children tumbling tearfully in her wake.

She ran up to the strangled man, lifted his head and breathed a sigh of relief. She understood nothing of what had occurred, but things seemed less awful than she had feared: the dead man was not her husband.

---

1. The choice, here, by Michel Verne, of the word "renounced" ("renié") seems to have a further New Testament connotation, in the sense of Peter, and Judas, renouncing Jesus in the Garden of Gethsemane, a possible Biblical echo which again inscribes itself into this novella's themes of wrongdoing, betrayal and remorse.

At the same moment, somebody banged on the front door and several voices were heard outside. Not knowing what it was that she was in dread of, Marguerite retreated towards the staircase, like an animal hurrying back towards its refuge when threatened by some imminent danger. She remained standing on the first step, her two children clinging to her skirt-tails as she continued to hold the third one in her arms.

From her vantage point, she could not see the cellar door. She thus did not see this door as it was pushed half-open, nor did she notice the head of Pierre Morénas, green with primal fear, worming its way out into the opening. But Jean, on the other hand, could see the scene in its entirety: the dead man, Marguerite and her children beating a hasty retreat and Pierre, his brother—a killer!—lying in wait in his hiding place and feeling the threatening approach of the punishment which follows close on the heels of a crime. In Jean's brain, thoughts swirled round in rapid succession. He`finally understood.

Pierre's presence, his terrible crime committed this day, the unfinished accusation of Uncle Sandy; all shed new light on past events. Today's murderer was the murderer of the past, and it was for the crimes of his guilty brother that the innocent man had paid. Following the murder of Uncle Sandy—and after the passing of time had caused the repercussions of the tragedy to die down—Pierre had come back, won Marguerite's heart and had, for a second time, destroyed the happiness of the wretched man who lived in despair under the brutal regime of the prison guards.

Ah, but… ! All that was about to come to an end! Jean had only to utter one word in order to overturn this accumulation of vile deeds and to get his revenge, in one fell swoop, for all of the tortures and humiliations he had suffered. One word? Not even that. He need only remain silent, and vanish quietly, in the same way as he had arrived. The killer could not escape; he had been well and truly caught. It would not be long before he, too, would experience the penal colony.

And afterwards?…

That word, Jean heard it as if a mocking opponent had spoken it into his ear.

Yes, really—and afterwards? What would happen when Pierre and Jean would both find themselves wearing the galley uniform? Would that restore, to Jean, his lost happiness? Alas! Would Marguerite have any deeper feelings for him as a result, and would she not still have loved this man who now trembled with the most cowardly terror? Because she did love him, she loved him with all her being, the poor woman. Her voice, when she had called out to Pierre, had rung out with her love for him. She continued to express her love now through her bearing: erect, hugging her children closely in her arms, obstructing the stairwell with her body, as if she wanted to prevent access to the household, defend it against some unknown yet keenly-felt danger.

At this stage, what good could come of informing on his brother? Would vengeance restore happiness to Jean—happiness which seemed, by now, impossible to attain? Would revenge save him from the despair he would feel from having also cast Marguerite herself into utter despondency? Was there not something better he could do: let the woman he loved continue to enjoy the illusion of her happy life, and keep for himself, the suffering, all of the suffering, to which, alas, he had so long been accustomed? To what better use could his bleak destiny be put? He was nothing now; could never again count for anything. The road was blocked before him, and there was no longer anything in existence which he might be allowed to hope for. To what better purpose could he put his useless being than to give it up for the salvation of another, another being who already possessed his heart, whose life would be Jean's life, whose happiness would be Jean's?

As these thoughts raced through his mind, people were struggling furiously outside, to gain entry to the house. The door was finally forced open, and four or five men burst in, ran towards the victim and lifted his head.

"Good God!" one of them cried out. "It's Monsieur Cliquet!"

"The solicitor!" exclaimed another.

They rushed forward. M. Cliquet lay outstretched on the table. Suddenly, his chest heaved and a deep sigh came from his lips.

The solicitor's face was sprinkled with cold water, and he quickly opened his eyes. Jean sighed mournfully. The murder attempt had not succeeded. As the victim had survived, it would only be prison for the assailant. Jean would have preferred the gallows.

"Who has done this to you, M. Cliquet?" asked one of the countrymen.

The solicitor, who was struggling to get his breath back, made a slight gesture to indicate that he did not know the answer to this question. He had not, in fact, seen his assailant.

"Let's start looking!" suggested another man.

In truth, they would not have to search for very long. The guilty man was not very far away, and moreover, he was about to hand himself over to his pursuers through his own stupidity: Pierre, hoping to take advantage of the initial confusion in order to run away, had opened wider the door which hid him from view, and had already stepped onto the tiled floor of the main room, ready to flee. There was no doubt but that he would be brutally seized and recaptured as he tried to make his way out of the inn. And even if he managed to escape this danger, there was a further peril which he could not avoid. He would, of necessity, have to pass in front of Marguerite, who had not moved from the first step of the stairs, where she stood as still as a statue. Seeing him, she would realize the truth.

The fact is, that saving the guilty man would have little benefit if Marguerite's happiness could not be saved at the same time. For this to be achieved, it was necessary that she should be able to continue to love the man to whom she had devoted herself; she must remain unaware, forever unaware, of the truth… Who knows? Perhaps it was too late… Perhaps a suspicion of the truth was already beginning to form behind the forehead over which had been cast the pallor of a mysterious horror…

Jean came out abruptly from the shadows projected by the mantelpiece of the fireplace, and moved forward into the light of the room. Everybody recognized him immediately: Pierre and Marguerite, who now stared at him, their eyes wide in astonishment, as well as the five local men, whose faces bore a complex expression, mingled with the friendship of the past and the unconquerable horror necessarily caused by the sight of a convict.

"No need to look any further," said Jean. "I'm the one who has done this."

Nobody said a word. It was not that they didn't believe him. His admission of guilt was, on the contrary, completely plausible, as a person who has killed before is capable of killing again. But this was such an unexpected development, that surprise paralysed the breasts of all present.

In the meantime, the details of the scene had changed. Pierre was now completely in view, away from the door; and, without anybody paying him any attention, he came close to Marguerite, who did not seem to notice his presence. She had straightened up, her face bright with both happiness and hatred: the happiness of seeing the complete removal of the suspicion which had momentarily crossed her mind, a suspicion which had hardly been formed before it was quashed; and the hatred she felt for this man whose self-confessed crime had caused her to even entertain this abominable supposition in the first place.

It was her; it was Marguerite alone that Jean now looked at.

The young woman waved her fist at him.

"You bastard!" she shouted.

Making no reply, Jean turned away and surrendered his arms to the firm grips which now descended upon them. He was led away.

The door, which was wide open, outlined a dark rectangular vista which Jean gazed at passionately. Against this dark background was etched for him the distinct contours of a bittersweet portrait: underneath the unforgiving glare of a deep blue sky, on a sun-scorched quayside, there came and went men carrying heavy loads, their feet weighed down with irons… But above them shone a dazzling image: the image of a young woman who held a little child in her arms…

Jean, his eyes riveted to this image, disappeared into the darkness.[2]

---

2.   In this poignant ending, the visual contrasts drawn by Verne, throughout this final chapter, between light and darkness, and between the mental image of Marguerite and that of the prisoners, seems to accentuate the contrast between Pierre's good fortune and Jean's despair.

Frontispiece for *The Astonishing Adventure of the Barsac Mission* (1914).

Foreword

Fact-Finding Mission

This unfinished novel by Jules Verne—the original French title of which is *Voyage d'études*—and which consists of four chapters together with the beginning of a fifth, recounts the arrival in the French Congo, and early days, of a nineteenth-century fact-finding mission, despatched officially by the French government. The broad mandate of this official delegation is to travel through this French colony, and to explore it from a political, geographical and economic viewpoint, with particular attention to the question as to whether the colony's residents -colonial settlers and colonized peoples--should be granted the right to vote at French parliamentary elections, and to field candidates at such elections. In Chapter II, Verne summarizes the principal goals of this fact-finding mission:

> This new expedition led by the engineer Deltour, should it succeed in achieving the goals of its fact-finding diplomatic mission, would result in finally filling in the current gaps in geographical knowledge and in completing the exploration and reconnoitring of this vast colony. A simultaneous outcome would be the definitive resolution of the question as to whether this colony should indeed send representatives to the French Senate and Chamber of Deputies in common with the other French territorial dependencies, an issue which would be resolved thanks to the two French members of parliament who had agreed to investigate the Congo with this question in mind, and who would leave no stone

unturned in order to discharge their mandate successfully. (Chapter I)

This story, though little-known up to now, bears all the hallmarks of quintessential Jules Verne literature—and, as such, forms a characteristic part of his "Voyages Extraordinaires dans les Mondes Connus et Inconnus" ("Extraordinary Journeys into the Known and Unknown Words")—in that it combines a fictional tale of travel and exploration, into exotic and dangerous locales, with much historical and geographical fact. It thus offers a detailed and exciting historical account of previous explorations of the Congo; much other historical and political scene-setting information on this colony, and detailed geographical information on the Congo's territories, climate and natural resources. All of this pedagogical information is interwoven with a fictional tale of exploration, one which promised, on the evidence of these early chapters, to be a typically Vernian thrilling tale of journey, adventure and danger. The reader is reminded of other popular nineteenth-century novelists who dealt with similar themes of adventure and exploration, such as H. Rider Haggard in *King Solomon's Mines* (1885). Africa itself had already been the locale for numerous Verne tales, including his first best-seller, *Cinq semaines en ballon* (*Five Weeks in a Balloon*, 1863), along with *Aventures de trois Russes et de trois Anglais dans l'Afrique austral* (*Adventures of Three Russians and Three Englishmen in Southern Africa*, 1872), *Un Capitaine de quinze ans* (*A Fifteen Year Old Captain*, 1878), *L'Étoile du sud* (*The Star of the South*, 1884; largely by Paschal Grousset), *Le Village aérien* (*The Aerial Village*, 1901), and *L'Invasion de la mer* (*The Invasion of the Sea*, 1905). Who are the members of this fact-finding expedition? Chapter III describes the leader and his fellow travellers. Monsieur André Deltour is a thirty-five year old highly qualified and competent engineer and seasoned colonial explorer:

He was a highway engineer who had graduated among the top students in his class, from the Ecole Polytechnique… and had already successfully carried out similar missions, in Sudan and Indochina, had established new travel routes and discovered regions that had been hitherto unknown, revealing them to business and industrial interests. (Chapter III)

He is blessed with an iron constitution, and with qualities of calmness under pressure, and courage in braving the unknown; in sum, a natural leader and explorer in the true Verne tradition:

> His temperament was one of unflappable composure, a coolness which could not be compromised by any possible occurrence; he had a high morale which no circumstance could ever lower; a level of courage which he had already proven on so many occasions, and, both soldier and scholar, he was the quintessential bold and daring pioneer of exploration, a model of those who had extended the field of geographical discoveries throughout the nineteenth century. (Chapter III)

The next member of the diplomatic mission is Louis Merly, twenty-five year old Secretary of the Geographical Society, who, in common with his leader Deltour, has strong reserves of courage: "A man of excessive boldness, [Merly] would be obliged on this mission to control his daring instincts." (Chapter III) Another quality which he shares with Deltour is his level of geographical and anthropological knowledge of the Congo and its native peoples, gleaned from his previous exploratory expeditions to this region: He "was as well-informed as it was possible to be, about the region, its geographical layout, its physical resources, the location of its different tribes and its native customs." (Chapter III)

The third member of the fact-finding mission is Nicolas Vanof, thirty-year-old Russian delegate of the International Esperanto Society and of the Esperantist Congress, described as "likeable, charming, extrovert, and passionately committed to the spread of the international language, Esperanto." (Chapter III) As we shall see later in this article, one of the significant subtexts running throughout this narrative is the importance of Esperanto as a means of attaining such colonialist objectives as furthering trade and spreading, to the French colonies, the imperial civilization. Vanof's role within the delegation is very much a linguistic, translatorial and interpreting one, as Esperanto is widely spoken at the time throughout the French Congo. Though Jules Verne does not specify a date in which this story is set, we must deduce from the importance therein of the Esperanto language, that this tale is

From the outset of the series, *Voyages Extraordinaires* (*Extraordinary Journeys*), the lure of African exploration had been a key theme, in keeping with the 19th century fascination with the continent.

set some time in the future relative to when it was written, since, in the French Congo of *Fact-Finding Mission*, Esperanto is widely-spoken, which was not the case at the time when Verne penned this tale.

During the sea journey from Marseilles to Libreville, administrative capital of the French Congo, Vanof has succeeded in infusing two of his fellow expedition members, Merly and Deltour, with his passion for and knowledge of Esperanto, so that, upon arrival in the French colony, "they spoke this language as if it were their mother tongue." (Chapter III) One wonders, of course, whether Verne is here employing deliberate hyperbole.

This story, in common with many other of Verne's *Extraordinary Journeys*, has its share of humor. In *Fact-Finding Mission*, much of the humor derives from the satirical depiction of the final two members of the delegation, its political and French parliamentary representatives, the deputies from the French National Assembly, Isidore Papeleu and Joseph Denizart. Verne's mocking portrayal of these two delegates contrasts sharply with his admiring depiction of the three foregoing members of the expedition.

Though we are told that these two politicians "enjoyed good health, being both blessed with an excellent constitution which... should render them eminently capable of enduring the exhausting trials of this expedition" (Chapter III), the narrator takes an ironic delight in describing the adverse effects of the rough sea crossing on these two men. Upon their arrival in Libreville, they are unable to join their colleagues in making a short speech before the waiting welcoming party and crowds who have turned out to greet the delegates, owing to the adverse effects of their *mal de mer:*

> Unfortunately… it was evident that they were not currently at the peak of their powers, ever since they had set foot on Congolese soil. It could be clearly seen from their pallid countenance and exhausted demeanour that they must have endured a great deal of suffering during the sea-crossing… [They have been, throughout the journey to the Congo on board the *Touat*] confined to their cabin, stretched out on a bunk bed, deep exhaustion having replaced the initial bouts of nausea. (Chapter I)

The deputies's sea-sickness is reminiscent of the suffering of the hapless Inspector Fix, as he crosses the sea during severe storms, in his worldwide pursuit of Phileas Fogg, in Verne's *Le Tour du Monde en Quatre-Vingts Jours* (*Around the World in Eighty Days*, 1873).

The relief of these two exhausted travellers, as they take a rest in their bedrooms within the official Residence of the Governor of Libreville, following their arrival, is palpable:

> "The thought of being able to spend a whole night in a bed which isn't moving about…!" added Monsieur Papeleu.
> "A bed where there's no danger of being woken up with your feet higher than your head!" was Monsieur Denizart's riposte. (Chapter I)

Yet despite their suffering throughout the voyage to the Congo, the two deputies are determined to persevere with their journey to the French colony, motivated by an overriding concern with appearances: "Perhaps, at that point, less dedicated travellers might have considered it necessary, in the name of prudence, to not wander any further beyond Senegal. But what would people have thought of them in their constituency and above all in their own local area?" (Chapter I)

Verne reserves his most biting satire for his depiction of the political leanings and "policies" of this pair of hapless deputies:

> being opportunistic by nature, always compliant with the latest and fickle swings in the tide of public opinion, they had nothing but friends across all factions of the political divide, and, should they have deserved any descriptive label amongst so many calibrated denominations of parliamentary idiom--conservative, progressive, nationalist, radical, radical-socialist, collective-socialist--it was well and truly the label "ministerial."... They were not given to debate or heated argument... and they voted with automatic regularity, unfailingly adding their blank ballot papers to the official majority; they were basically good fellows, helpful and inoffensive, the type of politician of whom one meets many examples... (Chapter III)

As to the opinion which the two politicians might have on the question of extending voting rights to the Congo's peoples, "The answer couldn't be simpler; they had not the slightest shadow of an opinion." (Chapter IV)

The narrator also mocks these two deputies for their unwillingness to make the effort to acquire some knowledge of Esperanto, which would have been useful to them throughout the fact-finding mission:

> neither gentleman felt especially inclined to learn Esperanto. They were the very essence of those fine French people, excessively patriotic, perhaps, who regard their language as superior to all others, sufficient to their communication needs in all circumstances... When they finally deign to learn how to say, in Esperanto, "How do you do?" and "Thank you very much indeed!," they claim that with those nine words... one could get around the whole world! (Chapter IV)

When the subject of cannibalistic tribes is mentioned to them at one stage, the deputies wryly reflect that "if deputies in Chamber didn't actually go so far as to physically devour each other, they did at least practise regular character and moral cannibalistic devouring of each other" (Chpater IV) Verne was himself a municipal councillor in the city of Amiens for many years, and one wonders whether his political satire is based on his personal observations from that period, just as, in *Jédédias Jamet or the Tale of an Inheritance,* a younger Verne satirically depicted the legal profession and its sometimes grasping clients.

The opening chapter of *Fact-Finding Mission* begins with the eagerly-anticipated arrival of a ship called the *Touat* at Libreville, administrative capital of the French Congo, in September of an unspecified year in the nineteenth century; this is the ship which has

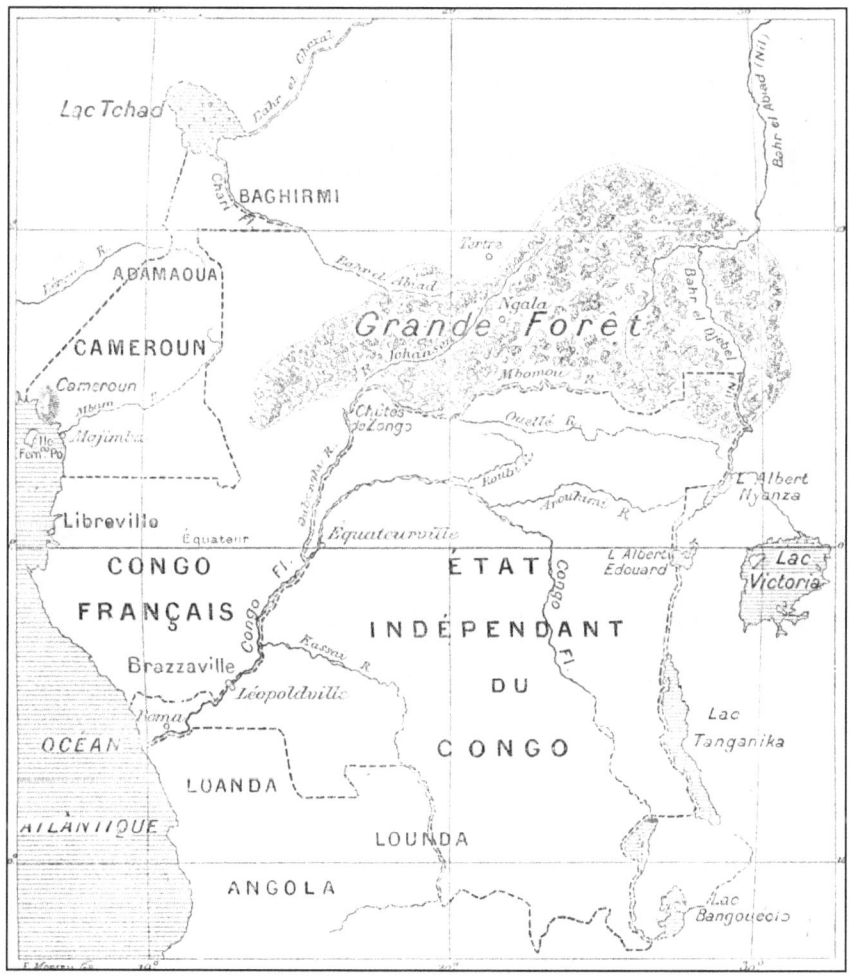

Verne's 1901 novel, *Le Village aérien* (*The Aerial Village*), had been set in the same region as *Fact-Finding Mission,* but involved a "missing link" tribe found in fictional "La Grande Forêt" (Great Forest).

brought the official French state delegation to the colony. The members of the diplomatic mission are accorded a hugely enthusiastic and hospitable welcome from across all the various national and ethnic spectrums of the multi-cultural community of the French colony.

> "There could be no doubt as to the feelings of the population of the city in reaction to this imminent visit, despite the diverse nature of its peoples. They greeted [the news of the visit] with joy… The Commission of this fact-finding mission could count on receiving the most friendly of receptions…" (Chapter I)

The Governor of Libreville thus addresses the warmest of welcoming speeches to the newly-arrived delegates:

> "Gentlemen… welcome to our colony, which is not unconscious of the interest which you are currently showing in it. It is aware of the purpose for which you have undertaken this mission, the outcomes of which will be so beneficial to this colony and which should further solidify and tighten the links between it and France…. Our colonists will do everything in their power to facilitate your task." (Chapter I)

One wonders whether this is another instance of Vernian comic exaggeration, and whether he is offering a somewhat "rose-tinted" depiction of unity and unanimous satisfaction with the colonial envoys, on the part of the residents of Libreville.

The tone of this narrative seems very much pro-colonization, with some references to the native populations bordering on the ethnocentric, as, for instance, the narrator's observation that "It goes without saying that, in the cities, the Congolese natives no longer circulated publicly in their primitive state of nudity. They all looked well in their light garments of cotton fabric…." (Chapter I) A pro-colonialist stance is evident in Verne's description of one of the native tribal chiefs who forms part of the welcoming party: "[He] was one of those remarkable members of the Bassoundi tribe, who have intelligent faces and upon whom the French administration could rely to develop and cause to flourish the civilization of this beautiful land." (Chapter I)

The Governor of Libreville is opposed to extending voting rights to the native peoples of the Congo, remarking that "it doesn't appear as though the vast majority of these native savages have yet reached a state civilised enough to be added to the French Parliament's Register of Electors…" (Chapter IV) He goes on to express further ethnocentric attitudes towards the colonized peoples when he remarks that native peoples should be allowed to vote only following inter-marrying with White people: "Unions and marriages between Europeans and native peoples are still too rare and we do not have, so to speak, in that vast region of the Congo, either persons of mixed race, nor quadroons, nor tintinclaires… nor any other offspring of the intermixing of the black race with the white race, though such miscegenation is especially the case in America." He warns the deputies of the danger of "one or two cannibalistic tribes people [being] returned to the Chamber of Deputies by universal suffrage." (Chapter IV) Verne appears to be satirical in his depiction of the racist views of the Governor.

Verne also gives much information on the tribal peoples of the Congo, contrasting the hostile tribes with the gentler natives. In Chapter I, the author offers a detailed description of the food and drink served at the official gala dinner, including much of the local Congolese produce, as well as of the many different indigenous flowers and plants used to decorate the tables.

Vivid, visual descriptions of the arduous journeys and harsh climate suffered by the various exploratory missions to the Congo are reminiscent of Verne's allusions to the burning rays of the sun under which the convicts work in *Pierre-Jean* and *The Sombre Fate of Jean Morénas*: "When, on the 19th of January, the expedition set foot in the first Muslim-occupied village of the Adamaoua, it was under the rays of a punishingly hot sun." (Chapter II) "The marchers walked on a ground upon which clay was mixed with sand. It was a roasting-hot surface, sun-scorched and sun-baked… by the fierce, burning rays of the sun over this Equatorial region." (Chapter V)

It is through the character of the linguist Nicolas Vanof that Jules Verne devotes much of this narrative to extolling the virtues of the international, artificial language Esperanto, as an instrument of attaining colonialist ambitions. The narrator advises us that this language has been invented in order to "foster easier communication between the peoples of the Old and New Worlds" and that, at the time

A postcard celebrating Verne, in Esperanto, appropriate given the theme of *Fact-Finding Mission*. Courtesy of Jan Rychlík.

in which this story takes place, "Esperanto had, for several years, been making deep inroads into the vast territories of Central Africa, to the greatest possible benefit of civilization and trade." (Chapter III) Though Jules Verne wished to use *Fact-Finding Mission* partly as a vehicle to extol the benefits to be reaped from adopting Esperanto as a universal language, there is no mention of this artificial language in Michel Verne's rewriting of this text, although he does preserve the idea of a city in which several languages are spoken.

Verne's use of language throughout *Fact-Finding Mission* seems deliberately grandiose and pompous, perhaps in keeping with the officialdom he is depicting. He thus seems to ironically mirror the highly formal, often frozen registers of political and administrative language, in his narration. His own immersion in the legal and political worlds at various points in his career, gave him an insider's view of such milieux, while his literary craft allowed him to mirror these worlds through language, fusing form and content.

The novel is left unfinished by Verne at the point where the expedition, accompanied by a sizeable cortege of porters and other helpers, is about to set off on its march through the Congo, in warm September weather. However, *Fact-Finding Mission* later inspired Verne *fils* to rework some of the ideas into a much longer novel entitled *L'Etonnante Aventure de la Mission Barsac* (*The Astonishing Adventure of the Barsac Mission*). This book originally appeared in serialized instalments in 1914, before being published as a full-length novel in 1919, with illustrations by George Roux.

The Astonishing Adventure of the Barsac Mission borrows the basic premise of an exploratory mission in Africa, as conceived by Jules Verne, but transforms it into a different story, with characters different to those in *Fact-Finding Mission*. It appears that when Jules Verne had begun writing the latter work in 1903, he had suspended his work on this story set in the Congo, due to shocking news reports of serious attacks against the native populations of that French colony. When Michel rewrote it, he thus prudently moved the action to the Sudan.

Prior to the time the real authorship of *The Astonishing Adventure of the Barsac Mission* was revealed in the 1980s, it was rendered into English in 1960 by I.O. Evans, in two volumes of the Fitzroy edition, *Into the Niger Bend* and *The City in the Sahara*. Because these books were published by Ace in 1970 as mass-market paperbacks, they remain easily available for modest sums on the second-hard book market. Hence, now with the translation of *Fact-Finding Mission*, readers can readily compare it with the work Michel spun from his father's idea.

FACT-FINDING MISSION

Chapter I

LIBREVILLE

On the date of the 3rd September of that year, a public notice was displayed at the entrance to the official Government Residence of Libreville. And here is what could be read, with obvious satisfaction, by the French inhabitants of that administrative capital of the Congo, as well as by its English, German, Belgian and Portugese residents, belonging to the neighbouring local commercial colonial agencies: (The fact that the text of this public notice was understood by all, is explained by the fact that it was written in Esperanto, that international language which, at that time, was becoming increasingly widespread amongst the population of central Africa. It is appropriate at this point to provide a translation of the text of the notice in question, word-for word).

The *Touat*, of the Fraissinet company, which has been sighted off the coast of Libreville, is due to lay anchor in harbour during the afternoon of this day, the 3rd September, at high tide, at four o'clock. The Governor General calls on the population to bestow the appropriately deserved welcome on the Commission members who have travelled here on board this liner. Two members of the Chamber of Deputies have agreed to take part in this official Fact-Finding Mission, the purpose of which is to decide whether this Colony should be represented in Parliament by a senator and a deputy. This decision has the potential to cause considerable benefits to accrue to the French Congo, and we thus urge the citizens of our administration to grant a warm welcome to this

Commission. The civil and military authorities shall proceed to the port in order to officially greet the Commission and to conduct it to the official Government Residence.

There could be no doubt as to the feelings of the population of the city in reaction to this imminent visit, despite the diverse nature of its peoples. They greeted, with joy, the news which had just been communicated to them. The Commission of this Fact-Finding Mission could count on receiving the most friendly of receptions, from the very moment of its arrival. Not a single discordant note would upset this harmonious concert. Moreover, the role of the Commission was clearly defined, and none of the neighbouring colonies need thus have any fear that it might wish to somehow infringe upon their rights: neither the Germans of Cameroon, nor the Belgians of the independent State; neither the Portugese of Angola, nor even the English, whose numbers were in constant progression throughout these vast regions of central Africa, need have any concerns.

Libreville, the current administrative capital, which could really be called the capital of the French Congo, had been occupied, from 1844 onwards, by those who had been emancipated. Built on the northern banks of the estuary of Gabon, it occupies the base and summit of a plateau which is dominated to the north-east by Mount Bouet and Mount Baudin, which are two hundred metres in altitude. The central group of houses and maisonettes is known collectively by the name of "the Plateau," and in the middle of these buildings can be discerned the Government Residence, whose massive structure, with its regular, even façade, forms a sharp contrast with the entire group of surrounding dwellings.

At this time, Libreville had begun to grow to an extent which boded well for its future, and it stretched over a length of more than seven kilometres along the harbour. Over the last few years, the figure for its population had doubled, to approximately three thousand white and Senegalese inhabitants. Having remained the colony's centre of military domination, and the city in which the Governor General resided, its importance continued to grow daily. Surrounding it, in the bush region, and within the shelter of the dragon trees, there were a multiplicity of bamboo huts of the Mpongwé region, in which there was a superb growth of coconut palm trees and oil palms. As for the

Catholic mission which had been founded close to the mouth of the Gabon, it numbered, at that time, more than two hundred children who were being taught a trade, not to mention the French and Esperanto languages, which were of mutual assistance to each other in the facilitation of business dealings with the towns and villages of the interior of the colony. Towards the south-east, another establishment, at Baraka, also provided education in French, which was the official language. In actual fact, thanks to its position on the estuary, Libreville found itself in the happy situation of being the natural trading centre of the region, and commanded the route to the Ogooué, which formed the northern part of the Congolese colony.

From *Découverte de la Terre* (*Discovery of the Earth*, 1878).

That day, it would not have been possible to wish for more beautiful weather to mark the arrival of the Commission. Undoubtedly, during the month of September, the heat is still considerable along an arc situated several minutes above the Equator. But the heat would have been much more difficult to endure in the towns further inland within the region, in the middle of those immense plains occupied by the various native tribes. Here, at least, and especially thanks to the rising tide, a breeze from the open sea made the atmosphere refreshingly cool, imbuing it with its briny smell. A few clouds blocked the sunlight for a few moments at a time, and long cloths of shadow ran along the surface of the harbour.

The speed and diligence with which the local population hurried to follow the Governor's recommendations should not cause any astonishment. From every direction, there flowed to the harbour both foreign and local residents, men, women, children, all dressed up in their most ceremonious finery in honour of the envoys on their way from France. It goes without saying that, in the cities, the Congolese natives no longer circulated publicly in their primitive state of nudity. They all looked well in their light garments of cotton fabric, woven in a variety of designs and colors. But the womenfolk, as during the time of the colonial conquest, with their necklaces and other items of jewellery of solid copper, loaded their shoulders and arms down with weights which sometimes reached sixty kilogrammes.

The garrison had received orders to have their regiment in attendance, with their weapons on display, at the official disembarkation of the delegates. Shortly afterwards, one could see, issuing forth from the barracks, officers and soldiers of the Senegalese colonial infantrymen, Senegalese boatmen, sailors, dockers, fort troops and all of the members of the Congolese military service specifically recruited among the Bakalais and the Ossiébas, all ready to render the necessary military honours.

The entire staff of the Catholic mission was in attendance, and the employees of the local colonial trading posts of Baraka had also all wished to participate in this ceremony, which would no doubt be recorded in the annals of the occasions of ceremonial pomp and splendour of Libreville's history.

Shortly before three in the afternoon, just as the waves were reaching the last change of tide, which was outlined by an unevenly-shaped line of kelps (seaweed and other types of marine vegetation), a cry broke forth from the waiting crowd which was lined along the shore:

"There they are! There they are!"

Although the *Touat* had not quite yet made its appearance round the turning point of Cape Joinville, one could at least discern the first furls of smoke blowing downwards in a south-easterly direction, heralding the imminent approach of the ocean liner.

The steamer, sailing at a rapid rate of knots, was quickly approaching near to the coast. Its hull was now visible, and those persons blessed with good eyesight could soon make out the guidons (small pennants used as a marker) at the head of the large mast and of the foresail mast. The French flag was quickly erected to decorate the ship's horn spanker. There could no longer be any doubt, then, but that this vessel, its stem reeling, pitching and swaying amid the white foam, was indeed the *Touat*, the regular mail boat serving Marseille, Dakar and Libreville.

It was not just the curious bystanders who were watching intently for the arrival of the liner. There were so many colonial settlers waiting for news of home, from such places as France, Belgium, Germany and Portugal! There were so many people anxiously and impatiently awaiting the delivery of so many letters, even more of which were awaited by recipients scattered throughout this vast country, in the local colonial trading posts situated along the banks of the Ogooué and of the Congo. Yet this latter group of recipients—and notwithstanding the fact that services of communication with the inland territories were now easier and faster—would not receive these letters for another week or even fortnight!

The bay of Libreville opens between Cape Joinville to the north and Fougère headland to the south. It is not easy to gain access to this bay. Wide shoals make sailing dangerous, including the reefs of "la Recherche" and of Milia, which, on the other hand, do also provide for safe and secure anchoring within the bay, as the swells from the open sea, which can be so violent in this part of the Atlantic, ultimately break against them. Moreover, there was nothing to be feared where the *Touat* was concerned. Its captain had an intimate familiarity with these waters, upon which he had been sailing for several years now. He could at this moment be observed, unhurriedly and unworried of mind, guiding his vessel through the channel between the reefs, and, at a quarter to four, he was dropping anchor at a depth of six fathoms, at a distance of two cable lengths from the coast.

From *The Aerial Village.*

As Libreville does not have an actual port as such, sailing vessels are obliged to lie at anchor, right in the middle of the harbour. A jetty—or what might more accurately be termed a wharf or landing stage—allows boats to berth in a smooth, trouble-free manner, and the disembarkation of passengers and unloading of merchandise can then take place without any difficulty.

The Governor and other officials had gathered on the platform at the very end of the landing stage. As soon as the French tricolor flag of the *Touat* was seen to symbolically salute the waiting throngs, the flag of the signal mast, erected at the end of the jetty, returned the salute, and, though cannon fire was not exchanged, at least the air was filled with the hissing of the steam which spurted forth in white curling scrolls through the valves of the engine and through the tailpipe.

Once the mooring and anchoring procedures had been completed, a small craft was lowered into the waters, and a number of passengers took their places in it; and, several rows of oars later, the craft had reached the foot of the landing stage.

The captain of the *Touat* was on board this craft; he was the first to climb the steps leading up to the wharf, followed by the five passengers who were accompanying him. Once they found themselves in the presence of the Governor, introductions were made by the said captain, in the following order:

"Monsieur Isidore Papeleu, deputy from Haute-Vienne; M. Joseph Denizart, deputy from the Lower Seine; M. André Deltour, engineer from Ponts et Chaussées (a prestigious French third-level educational institution of civil engineering); Monsieur Louis Merly, general secretary of the Geography Society, and Monsieur Nicolas Vanof, delegate of the International Esperanto Society."

M.H. Regnault responded with a handshake to the greeting addressed to him by each member of the Mission introduced to him. Compliments were exchanged, following which the cheers of the crowd broke out. The brief speech given by the Governor, on behalf of the authorities of the French Congo, was very short but exceedingly cordial, as was the official response of M. André Deltour, head of this Fact-finding Mission sent by the French government.

"Gentlemen," the Governor began, "welcome to our colony, which is not unconscious of the interest which you are currently showing in it. It is aware of the purpose for which you have undertaken this mission, the outcomes of which will be so beneficial to this colony and which should further solidify and tighten the links between it and France. It only remains for us, then, to wish that your investigations may proceed in the most favourable of conditions, and to assure you that our colonists will do everything in their power to facilitate your task."

It was the engineer André Deltour who officially responded to this welcoming speech, and his colleagues and travelling companions associated themselves with the expressions of gratitude which he addressed to the Governor. It is possible that Messieurs Papeleu and Denizart may have also intended to say a few words in their capacity as representatives of the French Parliament. Unfortunately, however, it was evident that they were not currently at the peak of their powers, ever since they had set foot on Congolese soil. It could be clearly seen from their pallid countenance and exhausted demeanour that they must have endured a great deal of suffering during the sea-crossing of the *Touat.*

It was indeed the case that, though the sea had been calm, and thus kind to the liner during the Mediterranean leg of its voyage, that is, between Marseille and the strait, as soon as they reached the wider ocean, the waves began to treat the passengers of the *Touat* more roughly, most particularly venting their ire upon MM. Papeleu and Denizart. Though both deputies had supposed that they could be justifiably self-congratulatory on being good sailors and on thus having the feet and heart of a sailor, at least between Marseille and Gibraltar, these congratulations came to an end as soon as the vessel was abeam of the long, heavy ocean swells whipped up by the violent Westerly wind which swept these waters of the Atlantic. From the Moroccan coast's Cape Spartel onwards, and until reaching Senegal, neither politician could enjoy the scenic views, the distant mountains, or the coast which was at times bordered by lush green forests and at other times as dreary and desolate as the edge of the Sahara. Confined to their cabin, stretched out on a bunk bed, deep exhaustion having replaced the initial bouts of nausea, they did not reappear on the deck or re-sight land until the moment when the *Touat* moored in Dakar Harbour. Perhaps, at that point, less dedicated travellers might have considered it necessary, in the name of prudence, to not wander any further beyond Senegal. But what would people have thought of them in their constituency and above all in their own local area? Elected Members of the Chamber of Deputies, who had officially requested permission to participate in this important mission, yet who had apparently given up halfway to their destination, all because of a bout of common seasickness! And what would, then, have been the point of their having gone to the trouble of becoming chosen in preference to a number of their colleagues, none of whom would have minded going off on an all-expenses-paid State excursion of several weeks duration, throughout the great Congolese colony! No! Their crossing was not destined to come to an end at Dakar, but rather, at Libreville, and so it was that, with brave resolution, they decided not to throw in the towel on any account.

When the *Touat* left Dakar, MM. Denizart and Papeleu had thus kept their seats among the passengers being transported to such destinations as the Ivory Coast, the Grand-Bassam, the Dahomey and the Congo. Their travelling companions, the engineer and the geographer, could only feel relieved satisfaction, as they had feared that this special mission, to study the colony from the point of view of its political future, might have floundered before even getting properly under way, in the absence of the two Parliamentary delegates.

Furthermore, the so sorely afflicted passengers of the *Touat* had grounds for hoping that the Gulf of Guinea might offer them a calmer sailing, and that the waters between the Cape of Palms and Cape Lopez might be less subject to the turbulence of the open sea; sadly, this was not at all the case. A great gust of wind even unleashed itself abeam of Fernando-Po, forcing the liner to change to an easterly direction, or risk being swept up on the coast. But twenty-four hours later, these violent gusts had abated, and the liner, setting back out to continue its original route, was finally able to lay anchor, and moreover, to do so in beautiful weather, at Libreville harbour.

Furthermore, it was at Libreville that MM. Papeleu and Denizart were planning to take the rest they so badly needed, over the few days which would be required to prepare the expedition. However—and as is usually the case—as soon as they had set foot on *terra firma*, and feeling more comfortable, they made themselves favorably visible at the Governor's welcoming ceremony, and it was on foot, taking their official place in the civic procession, that they were able to traverse the distance between the landing stage and the Plateau on which the Residence manor was built.

It would be no exaggeration to say that the entire population of Libreville was following in the procession of the authorities: the procession thus included European settlers and natives, both white and black, the latter being in a less primitive state than the era during which Monsieur de Brazza had discovered and conquered this vast territory, perhaps the biggest region of Equatorial Africa. Cheers and applause continued unabated, mingling with the sound of the rapid reports of musket and rifle fire. The curls of light gunpowder smoke unfurled into the air, while groups of startled birds fled in a flurry of feathers.

The Governor and his future guests arrived at the official Residence, escorted by the clamorous multitudes who continued their joyful celebrations until nightfall.

The two deputies and their companions were conducted to the bedrooms which would be theirs for the duration of their stay in Libreville, and their luggage, having been taken from the *Touat*, was quickly transported to them.

There can be no doubt, of course, that M. Papeleu and M. Denizart were in need of several hours rest. But how could they not partake of the ceremonial meal which awaited them, how could they not take their seats at the Governor's table, and how could they not deliver their official responses to the various speeches which would be made at that gala evening? At this moment, they had just sat down in the two adjoining and connecting bedrooms which had been placed at their

From *Un Capitaine de quinze ans* (*A Fifteen-Year-Old Captain*, 1878)

disposal. They had at least an hour to get ready, to freshen themselves up and don the sort of official regalia demanded by such occasions.

And the deputy of Haute-Vienne was saying, as he looked at his bed which was protected by the large mosquito-net which is essential in this region: "I could do with getting some sleep."

"I certainly could too, you know!" replied the deputy of the Lower Seine.

"The thought of being able to spend a whole night in a bed which isn't moving about…!" added M. Papeleu.

"A bed where there's no danger of being awakened with your feet higher than your head!" was M. Denizart's riposte.

But in just another few short hours, the two passengers of the *Touat* could enjoy a richly-deserved sleep, right until morning.

The official gala dinner was extremely well-organized and efficiently served. Several ladies from the European colony did honour to the occasion with their presence, and helped make it a lively, sparkling event. Two or three chiefs of neighbouring tribes took their seats at the Governor's table and were able to take part in the conversation whenever it took place in the Esperanto language. The menu comprised the main products of the Congo region: game dishes consisted of geese from the Zambezi river, cooked in wine and raisins, great-crested yellow grebe, an aquatic bird known as the "moganga," renowned for its exquisite meat, and antelope cutlets; the fish dishes consisted of silurids (a type of giant catfish), and a rare species of carp; vegetables included peas, lettuce, purslanes, yams, aubergines, "mioumbou," a type of potato, cabbages, tomatoes and red beetroot; fruits included bananas, "sokolobwés," which are drupes as thick as a coffee bean, which had reached complete ripeness at this season of the year, "sakombis" which were tiny figs, and which are the most succulent and tasty of wild fruits; oranges colored a golden-yellow, "ki-koundas" which tasted like grapes, and "mampotas," a type of prune with a delicious flavour; finally, drinks consisted of beer, wines from the Cape, the Canaries and France. It goes without saying that the freshest and most beautiful flowers adorned the table, all of the flowers of the bush region; haemanthus, strophanthus, dristarias, rhizomes, ficus, erythrinas, green cornflowers, gloriosas, proteas, "mioumbom," all of the powerful and varied floral products which were to be found under the rays of the African sun.

Truly, the delegation could not have hoped for a more favourable, warmer reception, and this friendliness which was being shown to it in the administrative capital of the French Congo would, similarly, be found by it in the other towns of the territory, as well as among the tribal peoples to be visited during the course of its fact-finding mission.

And even one of the tribal chiefs, Razzi, of the Kazembé of Kimongo, addressing himself to Deltour the engineer, made known to him in the following terms, the wishes of the tribes spread throughout the southern part of the colony:

"Noble chief of this expedition, on behalf of the natives of the Lower Congo, I ask you to be good enough to complete your journey, by taking a route through the regions of the southern border. When you leave Brazzaville, the quickest route will be to sail back down the watercourse of the Zaire as far as Loango. Between that port and the port of Libreville, the crossing is as short as it's easy. In this way, instead of simply retracing your footsteps, going back by the route already taken, you will have made a complete survey of the Congolese colony."

The native who spoke these words was one of those remarkable members of the Bassoundi tribe, who have intelligent faces and upon whom the French administration could rely to develop and cause to flourish the civilization of this beautiful land. He spoke easily in Esperanto, as that international language was currently more widespread in Central Africa than anywhere else, and could therefore be easily and naturally understood by all of the guests seated at the table in the Residence. It was only the two deputies who had to ask that this short speech be translated for them, a translation which was, immediately, duly provided by M. Nicolas Vanof.

As for M. Deltour, he thanked the chief for his invitation. He stated that he and his companions would do their utmost in order to comply with the chief's wishes, and that, all things considered, it certainly seemed as though this suggested return route was imperative, as it would allow the journey to be undertaken without danger or tiredness.

The meal was brought to an end towards nine o'clock by the warmest of toasts, after which the gathering continued for another while yet. The guests then retired and returned to their quarters.

From *Aventures de trois Russes et de trois Anglais dans l'Afrique australe* (*Adventures of Three Russians and Three Englishmen in Southern Africa*, 1872)

Messrs. Deltour, Papeleu, Denizart, Merly and Vanof now had nothing further to do but to return to their bedrooms, which they did after they have, one final time, shaken hands with the Governor.

As they sank into bed underneath their mosquito nets, M. Papeleu remarked to his colleague: "So, finally, we've got here; here we are in this famous Congo…"

"We may have got here, but we still have the return journey ahead of us," M. Denizart wryly responded, reflecting on the fact that, for the return journey just as for the outward-bound voyage, they could not use overland means of transport and that they would have no choice but to once more take to the open sea!

Both men finally fell into a deep slumber, for what was their first night of complete rest since the *Touat* had first set out into the waters of the Atlantic Ocean.

Chapter II

THE FRENCH CONGO

A lmost half a century has gone by since the original courageous pioneering explorers of the African continent, Speke and Grant (1857-1858), first penetrated into those vast lands collectively known as the Congo. In so doing, they were carrying on with a reconnaissance mission which had already been gotten tentatively underway by the Portugese explorers Almeida in 1798 and Graça in 1843.

It was in 1876 that Stanley, who had embarked upon a vessel which sailed along the Loua-Louba, reached the Congolese region, nine months after he had set out on his journey. In this epic journey from East to West, he had covered, in total, a distance of eleven thousand, six hundred and sixty three kilometres. He was the only surviving one of the four White men who had joined his expedition; he returned with only one hundred and fifteen men out of the three hundred and fifty-six people originally comprising his escort party.

In the year of Our Lord eighteen hundred and eighty—as peace had been reached between the foreigners and the natives—Savorgnan de Brazza arrived to occupy the military headquarters of Mfowa, a station which, having been evacuated, was shortly afterwards, reoccupied, in 1883. This army post, considered to be of the highest importance from a military point of view, due to its proximity to the great river and to the Stanely-Pool in the Ba-Lalli region, contained no fewer than five thousand inhabitants.

This superb territory belongs to France—and rightly so, since it was the most energetic of France's children who conquered it through their courage and perseverance. There were even some among them who had lost their lives in this enterprise which had been, so to speak, a superhuman one, fraught as it had been with all sorts of difficulties, and dangers at every step.

Following the first exploration endeavours made by Savorgnan de Brazza in West Africa (1875-1877), the illustrious explorer Stanley, who had already distinguished himself by means of his journey in search of Livingstone, through a southern part of Africa, reappeared in the Congo (1887-1889), when he was entrusted with the mission of locating the traces of the explorer Emin Pacha.

But the latter French explorer, who had landed in the port of Angola, which is situated almost at the mouth of the Ogooué, had already travelled back up that river, going ashore in such places as Lambaréné, Samkita and Sangaladi, visiting such tribes as the Okotas, Apingis and the Okandas at Lopé, and he had already founded a first establishment, which was a French general military headquarters in the Adoumas region, had stayed for a certain length of time at Nghémi, which would later be renamed Franceville, had continued his study of the regions inhabited by the Batékés peoples, and completed his exploration and reconnoitring of the basin of the Ogooué, which makes up the northern part of the region.

In 1887, the French explorer Paul Crampel, who had been mandated by France's Minister for Education to undertake a mission in Western equatorial Africa, set off, in his capacity as private secretary, with M. de Brazza, who was, at the time, the Congo's General Commissioner.

When the latter had to return to France, Paul Crampel, accompanied by MM. Biscarrat and Nébout, went to Lastourville with a contingent of Adoumas and Loangos tribesmen, and an entire freight load of cheap objects to be bartered. He left Lastourville to set off again on his travels, on the 12th of August, visited the regions inhabited by such tribes as the Schakés, the Bakotas, and the Obambas, went from the basin of the Ogooué to the basin of the Dilo river, reached Yébé, which is located slightly north of the equator, sailed back up the Ivindo, a tributary of the Ogooué, and made contact with the Ossiébas, who belong to the tribe known as the M'Fans or Pahouins. These people were a populous, important race, but were loud, dishonest and given to pillaging, and were a tribe of whom it was thus necessary to be wary and distrustful. After spending some time in the village of Bindzoko—a stopover necessitated by the fact that his band of fellow travellers were overcome with heat, their potential to continue their journey being thus significantly jeopardized by exhaustion—he continued onwards as far as Mount Koul, which is the farthest reach of French territory, and, on the 14th January, halted at the very sources of the Ivindo. Then, as he and his team had been attacked by the Pahouins, he had been obliged to retreat, returning in a westerly direction. Ultimately, it was only through his unprecedented, supreme efforts that he succeeded in reaching a military post flying the French flag, and was thus able to get back to the coast.

In April of 1890, Paul Crampel embarked on a second journey of exploration, going first to Dakar, a place from which he then set off again, landing on the 7th of May at Libreville. From there, he travelled onwards to Loango, and spliced through the long forest of Mayombé in a journey which was not without its difficulties and perils, and did not reach Brazzaville until the 20th August. From this city, he headed northwards and, having sailed up the watercourse of the Congo, launched himself into the waters flowing between the banks of its tributary, the Oubangui. The expedition then encountered a succession of obstacles in the shape of the tribes of the Bouzérous and Salangas, which had murdered the explorer Musy. Having spent some time at Bangui, Crampel and his contingent were obliged to cross the torrential rapids of Biri-Ngoma. Crampel and his companions were then laid low by disease. Crampel himself was afflicted by a raging

From *Cinq semaines en ballon* (*Five Weeks in a Balloon*, 1863)

fever, and it was in these conditions that, beyond the village of Bembé, he launched himself on a journey through unfamiliar territory, in the direction of Lake Chad. Along the way, he traded with the local tribes, the Langouassis, the Dakoas and the N'Gapous, finding himself among these peoples in May, and, finally, arrived at the settlement of the Muslim Snoussis peoples.

It was at this time that rumours of his death began to spread, this information having been relayed by one of his most loyal travelling companions, Monsieur Nébout, former head of Rufisque's harbour station. There were reports to the effect that Crampel and some of his fellow travellers had fallen victim to the savage native populations. And, after trying in vain to locate Crampel, M. Nébout had to continue his journey southwards and get back to Brazzaville.

It had already been a year since Paul Crampel had set off on his quest of exploration of the Eastern Congo, when the Committee of France's African Territories decided to despatch a new reconnaissance mission to endeavour to find the missing daring explorer.

M. Jean Dybowski, a French agronomist and explorer (1856-1928), who had returned from two exploratory trips to the Sahara, undertaken for the purposes of scientific research, was put in charge of organizing and leading this expedition, which would sail up the Congo and the Oubangui. He set out from Paris on the 9th of March, 1893, stopped over at Dakar on the 24th, dropped anchor in Libreville harbour on the 3rd of April, went onwards to Loango just as Crampel had done, and, like Crampel, led his fellow travellers onwards in the direction of Brazzaville, reached the military post of Loudima, then that of Comba, crossed the N'Djoué river with a boatman in a canoe, and concluded the first major leg of his journey at Brazzaville.

No sooner had he arrived in Brazzaville than he received, from the bishop of that city, news of a dreadful occurrence. That prelate had been in Lyranga, at the confluence of the Oubangui, when M. Nébout, who had arrived with about twenty Africans, had informed him that Paul Crampel and his travelling companion Biscarrat had been killed by the Snoussis tribe. A few days later, Nébout, the survivor of the Crampel mission, made a halt at Brazzaville, and the following are the details which he was able to furnish of this unfortunate event:

After giving up travelling by river, Crampel had headed towards the north, his goal still being that of getting back to Chad. In these

From *Adventures of Three Russians and Three Englishmen in Southern Africa.*

unsafe regions, and in the absence of a sufficient number of bearers of supplies, the difficulties were considerable. MM. Nébout and Biscarrat had stayed on temporarily with the Dakoas tribe whose members had hospitably accommodated them. It was there that, in accordance with the orders of the head of the expedition, they were to await his return. But as news of Crampel was slow in reaching them, Monsieur Biscarrat set off with half of the infantrymen and travelled a route which was shortly afterwards followed by a very worried M. Nébout. But the latter was only two days away from reaching M. Biscarrat's encampment, when he was informed that Paul Crampel and his travelling companion had been slaughtered at El-Kouti.

Though M. Nébout had by this time been reduced to only eighteen infantrymen and about thirty equipment bearers, he was nonetheless determined to march onwards towards El-Kouti. However, his men had refused to do likewise, and he therefore had to firstly return to the Bangui military post, then, having sailed down the Congo, he had just recently set foot on dry land at Brazzaville.

Such was the situation at this point: and what could Monsieur Dybowski do—not, any longer, to save Crampel and Biscarrat if it was only too true that they had been killed, but—to avenge their death? Get to El-Kouti! At this thought, he did not hesitate, and no matter what difficulties there might be in recruiting equipment bearers, as soon as he had succeeded in persuading M. Nébout to agree to march on El-Kouti, he got back on board the very gunboat which had just brought his companion back to Brazzaville.

Prior to undertaking this journey, it was considered necessary to explore several tributaries of the Oubangui, including the [M'Bali] and the M'Poko beyond the military outpost of Bangui, then the village of Yonka in the region of the Bouzérous tribe. And so, it was on the 8th October that the members of the expedition were, at last, all officially gathered together for departure, but only after M. Dybowski had first spent forty-seven days exploring the waterways of the rivers Ombella and Kémo. On the 23rd October, their preparations having been completed, porters hired and all provisions packed, they left Bangui to set off on the trail of the Crampel exploratory mission.

This new expedition, consisting of five Whites, forty-five soldiers and fifty bearers, set off in the direction of Bermbé. From the outset, Dybowski was gripped by fevers, but he did not halt his journey, so that by the 15th of November his small band of travellers was crossing the territory of the Dakoa peoples, and was already dreading the possibility of being set upon by those Muslim tribesmen, those Snoussis, the true perpetrators of the attack. On the 22nd of the month, the explorers reached the village of Pangoula, where they met with some Senegalese natives who had managed to escape the El-Kouti massacre.

It was, indeed, at this very location that the blood-soaked tragedy had taken place. On the 8th April of that year, Paul Crampel, borne along in a hammock, had just left El-Kouti to head back north. As soon as a first stop was made, his tent was invaded by the Snoussis who struck him with hatchet blows. He fell, succumbed to the attack, and it was thus that, in a despicable ambush, that valiant head of the French mission had perished.

M. Dybowski thus learned from one of his Senegalese informants that the Snoussis were prowling throughout this region. He wished to set off in pursuit of them, to avenge his two compatriots and to save those of their companions who might have escaped the El-Kouti attack.

But that village was situated two hundred kilometres from his current location. It would have been difficult to reach it even if he had sufficient strength of numbers, and thus it would be dangerous to not at all have the necessary number of people to overwhelm the enemy.

Therefore, despite M. Nebout's advice that they should march upon El-Kouti, M. Dybowski very wisely thought himself obliged to refuse to do this, and a resolution was made to return to the Bangui post. But it caused such distress to him and his companions to have been unable to avenge their fellow countrymen, and also to have been unable to give a Christian burial to the remains of the two victims!

But M. Dybowski had not given up on his original plans. Upon his return to Bangui, he was there provided with fresh supplies by a small steamboat, which was towing a larger boat which brought Dybowski new porters/bearers and various types of merchandise. It now remained only for M. Nébout to board this boat, on the 12th January, to return to Brazzaville.

The purpose of the Dybowski mission, as we know, was to firstly explore the watercourse of the Kémo river, a tributary situated to the right of the Oubangui. With this goal in mind, therefore, Dybowski took on board the canoes, with his companions, members of the Banziri tribe, one of the region's most loyal and also most intelligent indigenous peoples. He was able to reach the post of the Ouaddas within five days. But what difficulties he experienced in ploughing through the marshes and travelling across the Kémo's tributaries, as well as negotiating the territories of the Langouassis and the Togbos! He came to an agreement with their chief, Krouma, and took possession of part of this still independent territory. It was thus in these conditions that the important military post of Kémo came into being, situated a little above the fifth degree of northern latitude. A vast traditional tropical-style residence—the construction of which was contributed to by the help of the Togbos—now rose at the foot of the mountain, and, for the first time, the French tricolor flag floated in this region, and it was to be hoped that it would continue to float forever in this area.

When this building had been completed and then adorned by plantations of tomatoes and of papaya trees, these being types of fruit which were new to these indigenous peoples, for whom M. Dybowski had nothing but the height of praise, Dybowski headed back towards the post of Ouaddas, taking a new route through the territories situated between the Kémo and its tributary the Ombella. Once this part of the exploration had been completed, he then went back down to Brazzaville, where he met with a French explorer, Monsieur Maistre, who was to continue Dybowski's mission. Given that he was drained as a result of his fever, and overwhelmed by exhaustion, Dybowski knew that he absolutely must leave the Congo to go back to France. And so he left, once he had accomplished the mighty task of travelling upwards, in a north-eastern direction, as far as the line where there is a meeting of the waters of the Oubangui and the Chari, which is the main tributary of Lake Chad.

The fate of the Crampel mission, which M. Dybowski had been charged with finding and providing with fresh supplies, was now known in France. The Committee of Africa's French Territories had thus resolved to reinforce the strength of the second expedition. The leader of this third exploratory campaign through the Congo was,

Paul Crampel.

then, the aforementioned M. Maistre, who had returned from a two-year mission in Madagascar, and who was most particularly attracted to this new expedition, by his thirst for knowledge of the secrets of that mysterious African continent.

On the 10th January, 1892, M. Maistre and his companions, MM. Clozel, de Behagle and de Mézières, arrived at Bordeaux to board the ship to Africa. Having hired a certain number of local sailors in Dakar, they reached Loango, where the coastal colonial commercial agencies were in a position to furnish them with a contingent of four hundred bearers, whom they led in small caravans, towards Brazzaville, which M. Maistre reached after a thirty-day march. As has been said, it was there that he met with M. Dybowski, who was preparing to return to Europe. Two gunboats having been put at his disposal, M. Maistre resolved to reach the military post of Kémo as quickly as possible.

As soon as he arrived in Bangui, he appointed Monsieur Brunache as his second-in-command, as the latter had already discharged that same role during the Dybowski mission. Then, setting off in the canoes of the Banziri peoples, he reached Kémo after twelve days of journeying, just five months after leaving France.

M. Maistre's plan was as follows: to penetrate as far as possible in the direction of Baguirmi, to the north of the French Congo, in order to reach Lake Chad; and, should this prove impossible, he would return westward so as to reach the coast by a new route.

The expedition consisted of M. Maistre and his four fellow travellers; the escort was comprised of sixty men, of whom the majority were Senegalese soldiers armed with rifles and nine-shot *kropatcheks*, a type of repeating rifle named after its Austrian inventor. The expedition set off on the 29th of June. The initial stage of their journey entailed their having to cross the territory of the Ndris, an indigenous people who were, at that time, cannibals, and who are perhaps still so, to this day. Having negotiated with one of their chiefs, M. Maistre reached the village of Amazaga on the 9th July, and then set off deep into the bush country. Having already been deserted by several bearers and guides, and running low on supplies, with hunting yielding little food, he was attacked by the Mandjias tribe, to the sound of their battle tomtoms. Having managed to fight them off and cause them to retreat, not without substantial effort, he set up camp on the 19th July in a village he had come to, situated in the middle of a highly populated region in which his little band of travellers could stock up on fresh provisions. There, he was subjected to continuous alarmed warnings of imminent attack, and over a period of about twenty days, he had to fight against those savage Mandjias, despite the fact that this tribe was of the same ethnic group as the Ndris and Togbos. He finally reached the Gribingui which is part of the upper watercourse of the Chari. Would the expedition be able to continue journeying in the direction of Lake Chad? This stretch of water involved a perilous crossing, and on the 10th of September, M. Maistre halted at a settlement of the Akoungas, a fine hospitable people, who were sociable, and gentle in their ways. Indeed, throughout the entire journey across this region, the mission was always warmly welcomed. Agreements were negotiated with different tribal chiefs. On the 19th of September, the expedition arrived at the settlement of the Arétous tribe, travelled alongside the Gribingui as far as the mouth of the Vassako river, which, on the 4th October, the expedition managed to cross. This brought them to the territory of the Saras who accorded them a friendly welcome. The difficulty, however, was that of obtaining sufficient provisions. Finally, on the 10th October, M. Maistre and his fellow travellers met with the Bahar-Sara peoples. They then visited Dai, Sada, Koumra and Gangara, where they conversed with the native peoples of the Baguirmi and some of the government officials of the Bornou, in the territory of the Toumoks tribes. On the 7th of November, they set up camp at Palem, a town which had already been visited by the German explorer Nachtigal, and, finally, the expedition set off towards the Logone, one of the tributaries of the Chari, in the Gabéris region.

Moreover, any hope of reaching Chad had already been abandoned for some time now, and, as this scenario had been anticipated in his travel plans, it remained only for M. Maistre to return in a westward direction in order to get back to the coast. And, following a series of exhausting journeys and of great danger—two of his Senegalese fellow travellers having been murdered—on the 21st November he reached Lai, a city of ten thousand inhabitants, on the right bank of the Logone, a sort of capital city ruled by a Sultan chief of the Gabéris tribe.

The expedition left this city on the 27th, and, having then had to fight off various looters, it crossed the Ba-Tenna River, a tributary of the Logone, and crossed the high plateaux which form the watershed between the basins of the Chad and the Niger.

Jean Dybowski.

Having journeyed through the villages of Goudoumbin and Kaguenenga, of the Lakas peoples, they had to wander through the middle of a region in which water supplies were very scarce, before coming to the village of Lanné, which M. Maistre left on the 10th of January. In front of him, there stretched the desert which separates this region from the Muslim countries. When, on the 19th of January, the expedition set foot in the first Muslim-occupied village of the Adamaoua, it was under the rays of a punishingly hot sun. Beyond this village could be seen the outlines of the Bénoué valley, rich and fertile, which the expedition followed for five days, before halting at the colonial trading post of Yola.

This colonial commercial agency was situated four hundred kilometres from the coast, and as the tide was low, M. Maistre was unable to travel by the Yola steamboat. On the 4th of February, he was therefore obliged to set off once again on foot, and it took a month of travelling before he reached Ibi, a major British colonial centre established on the Bénoué. There, he and his companions boarded a sailing vessel on the 4th of March, and on the 23rd of that month they were greeted at the port of Akassa, at the mouth of the Niger.

This journey of five thousand kilometres—of which fifteen hundred kilometres had involved travel through unknown territories—had lasted, in total, fourteen months, and it was only on the 12th March, 1893, that M. Maistre and his companions set foot back on their native soil.

And thus was this daring enterprise finally accomplished. However, apart from the journey between Loango, Brazzaville and the Bangui military post, the expedition had, for the most part, taken place outside the borders of the French Congo.

This has been a description of the main itineraries followed with the objective of exploring this vast colony which, annexed with the Sudan, will perhaps one day form a great African state under French administrative rule. As we have already noted, the northern part of this region had been explored by the first (Crampel's) expedition through the Ogooué's basin. As far as the southern region is concerned, the other explorers, journeying from Loango to Brazzaville, had studied that route which runs alongside the southern border, an area usually frequented by travellers in caravans. As for the Eastern territory, there was no longer any point whatsoever of this frontier left undiscovered, a border region in which so many different ethnic groups live side-by-side, and in which so many villages are to be found, one after the other; this degree of exploratory knowledge had been achieved, thanks to the endeavours made to ascend in a northerly direction through travelling upriver by the Congo and the Oubangui. However, on the whole, within the depths of these territories and amongst the various ethnic tribes, some of whom are still at the most primitive state of savagery, the explorers were still limited to having made the most insignificant of conquests, and were still dependent on the accounts of caravaneers, and of arms dealers who had contacts with certain tribal chiefs. It can thus be fairly stated that researching geographers continued to lack official documentation.

And indeed, the territorial expanse of the French Congo is certainly considerable, bounded as it is to the north by the German Cameroon, delimited to the south by the Portugese Angola and separated from the independent region of the Congo—which has been, for several years now, under the authority of the King of Belgium with Léopoldville as its capital—by the great river and its main tributary. The number of

From *The Aerial Village*.

indigenous tribes populating the French Congo is very high, as is the population of villagers, be they settled or nomadic, who come together in vast, built-up urban settlements of between two thousand and five thousand dark-skinned inhabitants. In actual fact, it is estimated that there are no fewer than one million Congolese peoples spread throughout the land mass of this African region.

And in fact, this new expedition led by the engineer Deltour, should it succeed in achieving the goals of its fact-finding diplomatic mission, would result in finally filling in the current gaps in geographical

From *L'Étoile du sud* (*The Southern Star*, 1884).

knowledge and in completing the exploration and reconnoitring of this vast colony. A simultaneous outcome would be the definitive resolution of the question as to whether this colony should indeed send representatives to the French Senate and Chamber of Deputies in common with the other French territorial dependencies, an issue which would be resolved thanks to the presence of the two French members of parliament who had agreed to investigate the Congo with this question in mind, and who would leave no stone unturned in order to discharge their mandate successfully.

During this historical period, the four main cities of the Congo were Libreville, Lastourville, Franceville and Brazzaville; the first of these was located at the mouth of the Gabon, the last on the banks of that great river, with the two remaining cities situated inland.

It had thus been decided that M. Deltour and his fellow delegates would not travel by the same route already taken on several previous occasions between Loango and Brazzaville. Upon leaving Libreville, the delegation would cross the Ogooué basin, and would then set off in a south-easterly direction in order to reach Lastourville and Franceville. From there, by travelling downriver on the Alima, it would reach its tributary with the Congo which would bring it on to Brazzaville. Finally, the return journey would be made by the Loango route, thus acceding to the request which had just been formulated by the tribal chief Kazembé Razzi during the Governor General's reception.

Undoubtedly, the means of travel and communication throughout this region were now easier than during the period when such explorers as Crampel, Dybowski and Maistre had ventured into those territories at the risk of losing their lives. Nevertheless, there would still be significant trials awaiting the delegates, caused by such factors as the harsh climate, difficulties in pursuing an onward journey across land and water, and by the hostile nature of certain indigenous tribes. Notwithstanding these challenges, the plans for this journey had been carefully and judiciously studied and elaborated beforehand, and neither M. Deltour nor any of his fellow travellers were in any way lacking in either energy, daring or courage, and they would be well-placed to worthily accomplish their adventurous mission as befitted their fine personal qualities.

Chapter III

The Leader and His Fellow Travellers

The leader of the expedition, an enterprise which was to be carried out under the protection of, and with the assistance of, the French government, M. André Deltour, was at that time, thirty-five years old. He was a highway engineer who had graduated among the top students in his class, from the Ecole polytechnique, a prestigious French third-level training institute for engineers, and had already successfully carried out similar missions, in Sudan and Indochina, had established new travel routes and discovered regions that had been hitherto unknown, revealing them to business and industrial interests. His health was so excellent as to be resistant to all types of hardships, thus allowing him to brave the unhealthiness of those climates which had proved so lethal to so many other explorers. His temperament was one of unflappable composure, a coolness which could not be compromised by any possible occurrence; he had a high morale which no circumstance could ever lower, a level of courage which he had already proven on so many occasions, and, both soldier and scholar, he was the quintessential bold and daring pioneer of exploration, a model of those who had extended the field of geographical discoveries throughout the nineteenth century. Admittedly, the work which he was about to undertake within already-visited regions entailed neither extreme danger nor onerous responsibilities. Nevertheless, certain complications or difficulties could present themselves in the course of this expedition, which would require, for their resolution, the intervention of the brain and strength of a natural leader; but, in this regard, André Deltour's travelling companions could have every confidence in him.

Let us describe, briefly, this leader of the mission which had been despatched to the French Congo: he was a man of medium build, with a reliable and capable head on his shoulders, hair which was chestnut brown, close-cropped and strong, a lightly tapered moustache, a high brow, somewhat thin on top, a face which manifested, in its bearing, all the characteristics of a strong resolve, bright eyes with steady, hardly moving eyelids, wide-shouldered and wide-chested, of a vigorous constitution, with strong physical and moral resistance to hardship and exhaustion, endowed with that imperturbable calmness which nothing could astonish or surprise, and sparing of word and gesture. The Minister could not have made a better choice, given the objectives of this fact-finding mission, which had both a political and economic dimension.

The Secretary of the Geographical Society, who loved these expeditions to far-flung destinations, was no more than twenty-five years of age; a fine fellow, very experienced in all types of physical exercise, such as horse-riding, rowing, cycling, royal tennis played on an open-air court, modern tennis, and football. Indeed, his bicycle formed part of the expedition material, and he would most certainly find good use for it when the roads, which are still very basic, allowed the use of a bicycle, or if some unforeseen circumstance necessitated his being transported quickly from one point to another. A man of excessive boldness, he would be obliged on this mission to control his daring instincts.

"And when I imagine," he would say, "that one day, these hardly passable roads, these vast plains of the deep country will be travelled upon by cars travelling at a speed of one hundred and forty an hour, it makes me sorry to have been born half a century too soon, or not to be born half a century later!"

Needless to say, Louis Merly was as well-informed as it was possible to be, about the region, its geographical layout, its physical resources, the location of its different tribes and its native customs. There was nothing he did not know about the previous campaigns conducted by such explorers as Crampel, Dybowski, Maistre and indeed of all those who, over a period of fifty years or so, had contributed to unravelling the mysteries of this African territory, which had now permanently become a French colony.

M. Isidore Papeleu was an elected representative of the Haute-Vienne region at the French parliament, and his colleague in the French National Assembly, M. Joseph Denizart, represented the Lower Seine department. The former, aged forty-two, was tall, long-legged, lean and bony, with greying hair, though his goatee beard and moustache were still of a dark hue which owed nothing to modern cosmetics; his eyes were sufficiently short-sighted to require the use of a pince-nez in order to read or write, though not at all in order to direct others. As for the latter, he could not have competed in size with his colleague, being at least six inches shorter than him, and, moreover, was already encroached upon by a significant degree of portliness. In any case,

From *Clovis Dardentor* (1896).

if there was a similarity between these two members of the French parliament, it was in the fact that they both enjoyed good health, being both blessed with an excellent constitution which, consequently, should render them eminently capable of enduring the exhausting trials of this expedition under the leadership of the engineer André Deltour.

But if there was no physical resemblance between these two personages, there were similarities in their character which must, of necessity, have brought them together. Thus, ever since they had first entered Parliament, they had become linked by the bond of a close friendship which no circumstances could ever cause to deteriorate, nor any difference of opinion ever break the connection. It mattered little that one of them came from the Haute-Vienne department while the other represented the Lower Seine, the latter having Norman blood, while the former had Limousin blood coursing through his veins: they had been Parisians for the past ten years, to the greatest permissible extent, without, for all that, neglecting the interests of their constituents. Furthermore, those electors could never have reason to complain about these two deputies, so obliging were they, so kind, considerate, so devoted to their mandate, and always perfectly disposed to render service. Indeed, being opportunistic by nature, always compliant with the latest and fickle swings in the tide of public opinion, they had nothing but friends across all factions of the political divide, and, should they have deserved any descriptive label amongst so many calibrated denominations of parliamentary idiom—conservative, progressive, nationalist, radical, radical-socialist, collective socialist— it was well and truly the label "ministerial." Yes! Isidore Papeleu and Joseph Denizart were ministerial through and through, everywhere and always. They were not given to debate or heated argument, they never climbed to the heights of the parliamentary rostrum in order to address the House, and they voted with automatic regularity, unfailingly adding their blank ballot papers to the official majority; they were basically good fellows, helpful and inoffensive, the type of politician of whom one meets many examples, in different parliamentary centres.

For quite a number of years now, these "fact-finding missions" had been very much in fashion—if such a term is appropriate in this context. Members of Parliament willingly took part in them. The newspapers, most irreverently, called these missions "trips at the Princess's expense," and, though the coffers of that generous and noble lady were not always full to overflowing, these excursions continued, without fail, to take place in the most pleasant of conditions for their participants: transport in special trains, navigation on board State vessels, sumptuous receptions in the regions visited, and any number of ceremonial distinctions. But on the whole, there did flow from these various missions, advantages which were by no means to be scorned, and which were beneficial to the public interest.

It was, specifically, the African continent which had acted as the arena of these expeditions, which had been made to Algeria, to Egypt, to Tunisia and even to Morocco, and certain senators and deputies had fought over the government's invitations to take part in these missions. And so it had now come about that an exploratory mission of this nature was going, for the first time, to take place among the main towns and native villages of the French Congo. The mandate of this mission was not only to observe the country from geographical, ethnic and economic standpoints, but, as has been seen, to also study the question of political representation, and to decide whether the new colony should be empowered to elect representatives to the French National Assembly, just as the other colonies had been authorized to do. This is what the colonial settlers were seeking, and it was now timely and appropriate to examine the question of whether their demands should be adhered to.

And it so happened, in fact, that, for some time now, Isidore Papeleu and Joseph Denizart had been secretly nurturing a plan to become involved in some mission of this sort.

"It must be very pleasant to be able to see the region as a member of an official commission," the deputy of the Lower Seine would happily and repeatedly observe, "and without having to worry about the thousand minute details of organizing the trip."

"That's why I think we ought to avail of the earliest possible opportunity to discuss it with the Minister," was the habitual reply of the deputy for the Haute-Vienne department.

"Who will ask nothing better than to be agreeable to our request," Isidore Papeleu would assert, "since there are talks of organizing, in the near future, a fact-finding mission throughout the vast region of the French Congo."

"A strange region if ever there was one, given its location and customs!," cried Joseph Denizart, "and whose inhabitants, our fellow countrymen in agreement with the native tribal leaders, aspire to

From *Mirifiques aventures de Maître Antifer* (*Wonderful Adventures of Master Antifer*, 1894).

parliamentary representation. That means that there's a need to carry out an in-depth investigation of this region, which is possibly comparable to our French Algeria. From this flows the necessity for the members of the mission to travel through the different cities within the colony and to make contact with the numerous peoples spread across its territory. So it seems to me that the presence of several deputies or senators on this mission is highly advisable."

"I think so too," replied Isidore Papeleu, "and even in the event that there might be some type of danger to face."

"We would have no hesitation in braving any such danger!" Joseph Denizart courageously declared.

And so both men had already set out, in their imagination, and were launched across the long Congolese plains, penetrating deep within the depths of the African bush, sailing up the region's watercourses by canoe, swept along by the rapids of the great river and its tributaries, and thus finally bringing to fruition, and for the benefit of France, this glorious expedition!

And it was in this way that, upon their most earnest entreaties, the deputy of the Lower Seine and the deputy of the Haute-Vienne were, with the agreement of the Minister for Commerce, appointed to form part of the mission which had just been organised under the leadership of M. André Deltour.

But at the same time as Messrs. Isidore Papeleu and Joseph Denizart were granted ministerial authorization to study the region from a political viewpoint, M. Nicolas Vanof, member of the Touring Club and a delegate of the Esperantist Congress, was accorded the same privilege.

M. Nicolas Vanof was Russian, thirty years old, likeable, charming, extrovert, and passionately committed to the spread of the international language, Esperanto. It would be difficult to properly conceive of the extent of the zeal with which this passionate advocate—if such a term is appropriate—of Esperanto devoted himself to the language invented by Doctor Zamenhof, a language which Vanof had contributed so much to spreading amongst the Slavic peoples, tirelessly modelling himself on such persons as Cart, Beaufront, Delfour and other enthusiasts of a language intended to foster easier communication between the peoples of the Old and New Worlds. As we know, Esperanto had, for several years, been making deep inroads into the vast territories of Central Africa, to the greatest possible benefit of civilization and trade.

And it was quite something to hear the enthusiastic Vanof when, delivering lecture after lecture, he travelled from one place to the next, beating a path through the various countries of Europe, as crowds of listeners sat rapt at his fiery eloquence, conveyed sometimes through the medium of French, at other times through German, or English, and also through that Esperantist idiom which was becoming increasingly widespread.

"No, gentlemen," he would repeat in his vibrant tones, "no, this is not a language destined to disappear after a few vain attempts at spreading it, as was the case with Volapuk." (This was another artificial language, created in 1879, and which had met with a certain degree of success prior to the appearance of Esperanto). There can be no possible connection between Volapuk and Esperanto! That former language, the work of Doctor Johann Schleyer, was never viable from the outset! It was necessary to be a philologist in order to provide the world with a new language accessible to all, and the good doctor was merely a polyglot! He was guided by nothing more than his whims and passing fancies in transforming the most familiar roots, and as regards inflexions, he went about modifying them in so trivial a manner, that the roots and inflexions, linked in so illogical a fashion, quickly became unrecognizable."

"And consider his reasoning at the moment when he decided to christen his new language with that name *Volapuk*! How does he proceed? "Vol" comes from the English "world," or "monde" as it is called in French, and "puk" similarly comes from the English "speak," which means "parler" in French, hence Volapuk, meaning *universal language*. Now, while such combinations of words might be sufficient for the Saxon races, the Latin races no longer understand anything of them, in which case, we must ask what then becomes of that much-needed project of linguistic internationalisation, which aspires to penetrating as far as the farthest-flung regions of the world, and whose natural meanings should be understandable by all persons!"

"This is not the case with Esperanto, and all of you who are here listening to me at this moment, understand it as well as if I were speaking to you in your native language, as it (Esperanto) is formed from roots borrowed from various different languages. Does this not explain how, over the past twenty years or so, it has succeeded in making its mark in the New World as well as in the Ancient World? And don't you know that, in Europe alone, it is spoken fluently in Austria, Hungary, Switzerland, Germany, England, France, Belgium, Bohemia, Bulgaria, Denmark, Finland, Sweden, Norway, Spain, Italy, Holland, Russia, Moravia, Portugal, Turkey...! And just imagine that it has had no trouble crossing the oceans! Travel to America, Africa, the South Sea Islands, and you will find, everywhere, Esperantists to understand you when you shall speak Esperanto! Esperanto is the surest and most rapid vehicle of civilization!"

From *The Aerial Village*.

This is an example of how Nicolas Vanof would express himself. And in truth, for a language to spread worldwide, it is not enough to label it a world language. "Pork e lingvo estu universala, ne suficas doni al gitian nomon."

That was the epigraph contained on the pamphlet written by Doctor Louis Lazare Zamenhof, who originally came from a city of the Grodno government, of the Russian Empire. In that city, called Bieloskok (now in Poland), which had a very varied population, inhabited as it was by Russians, Poles, Germans and Hebrews, and in which four languages were spoken, there reigned a lamentable confusion of tongues, to such an extent that people could simply not manage to understand each other. It was undoubtedly this circumstance which gave Doctor Zamenhof his brilliant idea, the culmination of which was celebrated on the 5th December, 1878.

That pamphlet had been the good doctor's first publication. It began with an interesting preface which highlighted the advantages of an international language, the various facets of the linguistic problem which needed to be resolved, and the manner in which such a resolution would be brought about. Next appeared a number of quotations, in both prose and verse, followed by the grammatical rules of Esperanto; and finally, there was a dictionary comprising nine hundred fundamental roots.

This was how the structure of the publication was described in his specialist journal by a zealous supporter of the Russian doctor, a certain Monsieur de Beaufront, manager and editor of this powerful instrument of promotion of the cause of Esperanto.

It is, moreover, appropriate to point out that the study of Esperanto did not entail any difficulties in pronunciation or memorisation. One learns it as naturally as one breathes, if you will allow me to use that somewhat trite expression. After ten lessons, students are capable of conversing with each other. There has even been published a booklet entitled *Esperanto in Ten Lessons* (*Esperanto in dos lecciones*). It should therefore come as no surprise to learn that, at the present time, the number of its adherents throughout the whole world amounts to more than one hundred thousand. And it is only right that we should not at all forget that it is thanks to the association known as the Touring-Club of France, to its continuous encouragement, its numerous publications and its co-operation, given in every possible form, that the new international language has experienced a degree of growth which is as rapid as it is wonderful.

It is necessary to observe that Esperanto is a simple, adaptable, harmonious language, lending itself equally well to the elegance of prose and the harmony of verse. It is capable of expressing all thought, and even the most exquisite feelings of the soul. Furthermore, through its constituent elements, it is the international language *par excellence.* The masterful and central concept which regulated its formation is the choice of roots in accordance with their degree of international familiarity, that is, chosen by universal franchise, as it were.

As regards pronunciation, in order to make it easier for the masses to absorb, Doctor Zamenhof took care to align phonetics with script in choosing international linguistic elements.

The only objection that could be made is that the Swedes and Russians have languages which are farther removed from Esperanto, from the point of view of pronunciation, than the other languages of Europe. In this regard, therefore, they must make a greater effort than Latin or Anglo-Saxon peoples. And yet, Esperanto is of such practical usefulness that Russia contains the greatest number of its practitioners, while Sweden is in second place for the number of speakers of Esperanto.

From *Sans dessus dessous* (*Topsy-turvy*, 1889).

In this way, Esperanto has set down deep and thriving roots in every country: to such an extent, we can proudly state—and France has made the greatest contribution to this achievement—that there are no longer any regions in existence where there are no Esperantists to be met with.

Such were the results currently obtained by the passionate disseminators of Esperanto, and we must now return to the significant progress that they had made in Central Africa. In his capacity as delegate of the Touring-Club, Nicolas Vanof was about to determine the extent of this progress, firstly in this large colony of the French Congo, before, secondly, extending his research to the Independent Congo, at the instigation of the *Belga Sonivolo,* the Belgian journal of Esperanto.

From *Adventures of Three Russians and Three Englishmen in Southern Africa,*

With such a zealous advocate of the cause on board, one should not be unduly surprised to learn that, throughout the sea crossing of the *Touat* between Marseille and Libreville, the issue which was most frequently discussed was, precisely, the Esperantist question. The engineer André Deltour, and Louis Merly, had asked nothing better than to learn a language from which they would derive great benefit throughout the planned expedition. With a teacher who burned with such enthusiasm, they were likely to make swift progress in this subject, and this is indeed the result which was achieved without difficulty. During the long periods of free time throughout the sailing, Nicolas Vanof was able to inculcate them with the grammatical principles and vocabulary of Esperanto. Thus, upon their disembarkation onto African soil, they spoke this language as if it were their mother tongue.

And even other passengers on board the liner, industrialists and merchants, who were coming to set up business in the Congo, did not miss out on such a fortuitous opportunity to learn a language which would make their business dealings so much smoother. It was therefore akin to an actual class of students which sailed towards these Western waters of Africa. In truth, even if the entire crew of the *Touat* were not initiated into the structures of Esperanto, so easy and so logical, there were few such non-initiates, and it would not have been unduly surprising if, upon arrival in dry dock in Libreville, the captain of the liner had given orders in that tongue which, though commercial in origin, is also set to become a maritime language.

And so, as for the deputy of the Lower Seine and the deputy of the Haute-Vienne, were they not among the numerous and highest-achieving students of Nicolas Vanof?

Well, first of all, it should be pointed out that the sea had not proven at all merciful towards Isidore Papeleu and Joseph Denizart. Once the *Touat* had crossed the Strait of Gibraltar, they were hardly ever able to emerge from their cabin throughout the entire remaining part of the crossing, and on the rare occasions that they did so, what a pitiful state they were in! Most certainly, they would have been quite unable to acquire a taste for the study of Esperanto, any more than they could have enjoyed the varied menus of the dining room table. Professor Vanof's lessons would not have been digested any more easily than the dishes, no matter how well prepared by the ship's chef: the brain, just like the stomach, would have simply refused to co-operate. Therefore, the two honourable members of Parliament, upon arrival at Libreville, understood no more of Doctor Zamenhof's language than they had when they left Marseille!

And, furthermore, why not admit it, neither gentleman felt especially inclined to learn Esperanto. They were the very essence of those fine French people, excessively patriotic, perhaps, who regard their language as superior to all others, sufficient to their communication needs in all circumstances, and, even if they had been in possession of their full faculties, the two parliamentarians would probably have dispensed with attending Nicolas Vanof's classes, and they didn't even think about it, not even when they had set foot upon African soil. At that moment, in fact, they had only one concern: to recover, over the first few days, from the exhaustion of such a rough crossing.

However, during their stay in Libreville, they thought it fitting to somewhat relax their intransigent stance. And, as Nicolas Vanof unrelentingly insisted on the advantages to the mission of a knowledge of Esperanto, they replied to him:

"Very well… We agree with you, and if we had not been so unhappily indisposed on board the *Touat,* we would have ensured to benefit from your lessons… Moreover, you speak this new language, as do M. Deltour and M. Merly, and since we're not going to be apart from you, it's the same as if we too spoke it!…"

"All the same," Nicolas Vanof rightly pointed out, "some sort of situation could arise in which you would have to speak it yourselves…"

"Well then, it would be enough for us to know a few words appropriate to the particular request," declared M. Isidore Papeleu.

"And a few words appropriate to the answer," added M. Joseph Denizart.

And so it was that the two colleagues ended up learning to say in Esperanto "How do you do?" and "Thank you very much indeed!"

"With those nine words," they claimed, "one could get around the whole world!"

Chapter IV

Final Preparations

For the most part, the territory of the French Congo does not offer a very hilly or undulating landscape. The long, practically bare plains, which are arid, and ravaged by tropical heat, are followed by the deep thickness of the bush country, throughout which the traveller is protected from the burning rays of the sun, as he or she advances through the bush, by an overhanging dome or vault of great trees. Here and there can be found elevations of medium height, which are landscapes of hills more so than mountains, at the foot of which there flow numerous winding watercourses, which are virtually dried up during the summer season, but which are full to overflowing their banks during the rainy season.

Moreover, the two principal basins of the Congo's network of rivers, that of the Ogooué in the northern part and that of the Congo or Zaire in the southern part, form the two major divisions of this region. Therefore, throughout the expanse of the Congo, upon which there is still a penury of negotiable roads, and in which modes of transport are similarly lacking, trade can be carried out only by travelling in caravans, which take long months to cover the distance between the coast and the border to the East, departing either from Loango or from Libreville.

During that period in which the mission led by the engineer André Deltour was setting out to complete, if possible, the study of the Congolese colony, the journey was still fraught with the same difficulties as at the time when such men as Brazza, Crampel, Dybowski and Maistre had ventured through unknown territory. It was therefore advisable to proceed in the same manner as these original explorers.

There could be no question of bringing along horses, carts, or vehicles of any description, given the lack of roads on the one hand, and the lack of pastures on the other, throughout the arid parts of this territory. The caravan, organized by the head of the expedition, would thus proceed on foot towards the interior of the territory. It would cross the forest and the plains by degrees, in a series of stages; it would sail up or down the watercourses, upon which it would be transported either by the canoes of the natives, or by the steamboats and gunboats which are occupied, with varying degrees of regularity, in the navigation of the Congo and the Ogooué, and of the tributaries of these two rivers.

Needless to say, MM. André Deltour and Louis Merly had studied the region by means of the most authentic and most recent documented descriptions of same, benefiting from the different reconnaissance missions carried out before them by the daring conquerors of this important colony of Western Africa. Their first concern had been to ensure the safety of the mission throughout its long march, in the midst of tribes which had not been completely subjugated and remained savage. They then had to ensure that the members of the expedition were provided with sufficient supplies, as hunting or fishing alone would not have procured them adequate resources.

The following, then, is a description of the persons of whom the expedition was comprised, excluding M. André Deltour and his four travelling companions:

In anticipation of the planned expedition—to ensure its safety—a military escort had been organized through the good offices of the Governor General, Monsieur H. Regnault. It consisted of forty Senegalese infantrymen, and native canoeists, under the orders of two sergeants, Trost and Césaire. These two sergeants were natives of France; one was twenty-seven years old, the other thirty; they were excellent soldiers, serving within Africa, and had been, for several years now, part of the colonial military service; they were very much inured to the hardships of the climate, very vigorous and active, extremely resourceful, very experienced in the management of native troops, and their superiors could have complete trust in their zeal and devotion.

The infantrymen, solidly built, strong men, had been hand-picked from amongst the best-trained and most disciplined members of that special troop of soldiers, which was armed only upon order of the Minister for the colonies; such an order had been given for M.

From *The Astonishing Adventure of the Barsac Mission*.

Dybowski's escort. Their uniform consisted of a coat of dark woollen cloth, canvas trousers held in place by a wide flannel belt, shorts and a shirt of cotton fabric. Their headdress consisted of the red fez, the blue tassel of which came down as far as the shoulder.

In addition to this battledress, which had been well designed for a campaign of this type, the soldiers had weapons appropriate to the defensive precautions necessitated by possible encounters with certain tribes dreaded by the travelling caravans, tribes which were mainly to be met with inland. The Senegalese were, therefore, each armed with a kropatchek rifle containing a bayonet, a slicing sabre and a hatchet. To their back was fitted a type of rucksack, and they wore a bayonet-carrier and cartridge belt around their waist.

These men, under the orders of the two sergeants Trost and Césaire, and who had been held ready and made to observe discipline for the last few months by means of marches round the outskirts of Livereville, and by firearms exercises, were thus very skilled, accurate marksmen. Moreover, they were all the result of a choice of the best soldiers which their garrison had to offer, and they provided every guarantee of vigour and loyalty. Many among them had already proven their military worth during the course of previous expeditions.

The remainder of the personnel of the mission consisted of about sixty porters, recruited by foremen known as "capites" or "roundheads." These native carriers or porters, of materials for the expedition, are not at all paid in money but rather in merchandise, and they are assigned to the carrying of the material of the caravans, all personal trunks and cases, and hammocks in which the Whites take their place whenever they are forced to do so by illness or exhaustion, each hammock being carried by four natives, two in front, two at the rear. The expedition's material also consists of packages and bundles of merchandise, and of numerous crates and boxes of provisions which have to feed about one hundred individuals when they are en route between villages which are scattered over the territory, and which are thus separated from each other by long distances, amidst arid regions.

The merchandise to be used for trade or exchange with the natives, either as gifts or in payment, consisted of pieces of white and red fabric which are highly sought after by the Congolese peoples, of knives, mirrors, golden nails, copper wires and other assorted goods of, in some cases, admittedly varying worth and value.

As for provisions, they consisted of nothing more than barrels of bacon, canned meat and dry fish. After all, could the travellers not count on the products of the hunt, in the forests and on the plains, and also on fish caught, as there are numerous flowing rivers at this time of year, when the water supplies of the country's rivers have not yet been diminished or completely evaporated by the Equatorial heat?

Throughout the few days spent in Libreville, André Deltour and Louis Merly had closely overseen the organization of the caravan. Being very familiar with the difficulties of such journeys, and having learned from the experiences of their predecessors, they did not intend to leave anything to chance, and had no intention whatsoever of being caught off guard under any circumstances. Even though this mission was set to travel across the colony in more favourable conditions than had applied during previous expeditions, it was still necessary to take account of possible extreme exhaustion, possible deprivation and even of dangers posed by being amongst peoples who were still prone to rebellion; it was also necessary to be prepared for possible attacks by Muslims from the north-east. Moreover, there was no shortage whatsoever of caravan "hi-jackers," "highwaymen" and looters in these vast regions in which the inland villages of the territory are often some sixty kilometres apart. Besides, the Governor of Libreville had placed himself at the engineer's disposal in order to procure for him the safest possible documents of passage and to smooth the way for this eminently perilous task. Furthermore, and again thanks to the efforts of the Governor, the personnel of the expedition was to be supplemented through the recruitment of a guide in whom every trust could be placed.

This guide belonged to the Bakotas tribe, who occupy a region within the Ogooué territory to the east of Libreville. Aged about thirty, this guide, named Linvogo, accustomed by his upbringing and native origins to the climate of the colony, was robust, of an iron constitution, and of highly regarded intelligence; M.H. Regnault had already, in many circumstances, used his services without ever having had cause to complain either about his courage or his loyalty. Thus, for several months now, Lingvo had been part of the staff of the Government Residence and received a regular salary, which was provided for within the budget of the colony administration. Though he did not speak all of the languages used by the native tribes, and which often vary from one tribe to the next, he was at least familiar with the essence of the

Congolese language. And one thing which it is useful to point out, a fact noted with satisfaction by Nicolas Vanof, is that the guide was familiar with the Esperantist language.

These diverse activities of preparation could not but be of interest to the two parliamentary colleagues from the Palais-Bourbon. Furthermore, they relied completely on the head of the mission for everything connected with the details of this campaign. Moreover, the point of view from which they were to study this region is already known to us: was it appropriate that the Congolese colony be represented in Parliament by a senator and a deputy? This is the question which M. Isidore Papeleu and M. Joseph Denizart had to take account of and carefully consider, and, to begin with, their investigations would start at Libreville.

From *The Astonishing Adventure of the Barsac Mission.*

This proposed parliamentary representation was indeed the wish of the entire population, both European and native, and, concerning this question, might there not be rivalry between these two groups of people, each of which had a mentality so different from the other? There have been and there still are in both the Chamber of Deputies and the Senate, true mulattos, if not pure-blood Negroes. Therefore, why should such peoples as the Loangos, the Bakotas, the Adoumas, the Batékés or the Pahouins not put forward candidates of their color, a color which, this time, would no longer be political but social in nature?

What was the opinion of the deputies of the Haute-Vienne and the Lower Seine on this point? The answer couldn't be simpler: they had not the slightest shadow of an opinion. They would observe, study, consult, and encourage others to express their ideas. They would even organize public lectures and meetings in the principal cities of the colony—contradictory lectures to which all of the future electors would be admitted. However, as far as Libreville was concerned, there was no doubt but that the Governor M. H. Regnault and the civil and military authorities were opposed to this extension of voting rights to the different native races of Congolese ethnicity spread over the expanse of the region.

Most probably, in their heart of hearts, the two parliamentary colleagues must have been of that same opinion, that the right to vote should be granted only to those citizens who were part of the European population of the Congo. But as they were conscientious investigators, they would not reach a conclusion until they had examined the question in depth, and within the locations concerned, since their itinerary would allow them to visit the successive main colonial centres.

Nevertheless, M. Isidore Papeleu did ask M.H. Regnault:

"But why exclude all of the native population?"

"Why? Though the civilising mission has made significant progress in this country," the Governor replied, "it still hasn't adequately penetrated the settled or nomadic tribes, and it doesn't appear as though the vast majority of these native savages have yet reached a state civilised enough to be added to the French Parliament's Register of Electors."

"But all the same, surely," replied M. Joseph Denizart, "isn't it exactly the same situation at present in all the other French colonies, in the West Indies, Indochina, and, within African territory, in Senegal?"

"Without a doubt, gentlemen," declared M. H. Regnault, "but in those colonies there exists an intermediary class which hasn't yet had the time to become formed here in the Congo. Unions and marriages between Europeans and native peoples are still too rare and we do not have, so to speak, in that vast region of the Congo, either persons of mixed race, nor quadroons (the offspring of a Mulatto and a White, and thus, one quarter black), nor tintinclaires, who are the offspring of a Tornatros man and a Spanish woman, nor any other offspring of the intermixing of the black race with the white race, though such miscegenation is especially the case in America."

"Your reasoning on this matter is quite correct, Monsieur le Gouverneur," replied Isidore Papeleu. "But for all that, it's highly likely that we'll find ourselves up against debates with any number of complaining activists calling for full native representation in Parliament."

"It's indeed highly likely, *monsieur le député*; however, I must point out to you that Algeria has been a French colony for the past seventy years already, and, although there are no longer any cannibals to be found there, unlike here in the Congo, and besides the fact that Algeria is home to five million Arabs, it has never sent one of its own race as a parliamentary representative."

"Well, at the end of the day," concluded M. Joseph Denizart, "this whole issue will form the object of a very serious fact-finding research trip on our part, and our eventually produced written report on the subject, supported by personal observations, and to which we will give complete diligence and care, ought to certainly enlighten the Government on this highly serious question!"

"Moreover," added M. Regnault, "throughout the course of this fact-finding mission, you are will be initiating contact with the largest and most important tribes of this colony. You shall observe their customs, their mores, values, you will produce a deeply detailed description of their traditions and ideas, and you will thus be enabled to make your judgements in full knowledge of the surrounding facts. I reiterate, there do continue to exist cannibals within certain Congolese tribes; these people willingly eat each other; the victors eat the vanquished. And what would you have to comment if—and this is something that could conceivably happen—one or two cannibalistic tribespeople were returned to the Chamber of Deputies by universal suffrage?"

From *The Astonishing Adventure of the Barsac Mission.*

Exchanging a glance, the two colleagues seemed to decide that it was more prudent not to dare to reply that, though if deputies in Chamber didn't actually go so far as to physically devour each other, they did at least practice regular character and moral cannibalistic devouring of each other, so that opposing political groupings sometimes—metaphorically, at least—ate each other without salt! But, at the end of the day, they would not leave this country until they had studied this electoral question in all of its aspects, and until they had seen to it personally, neglecting nothing, that their investigation was as sincere as it was thorough and definitive.

Moreover, this opinion, this aspiration if you like, of the native colonised peoples to have their names officially inscribed upon the Register of Electors of the colony, had been confirmed to the two Parliamentary representatives during several visits to the chief Kazembé razzi, with whom they had a detailed discussion and conversation at the first reception hosted by the Governor. Quite naturally, Nicolas Vanof had been present at these visits, since the two colleagues spoke neither the Congolese nor Esperantist languages, the only tongues understood by the chief. Vanof had thus acted as interpreter between the chief and the Members of Parliament.

Razzi had been insistent on the point that the diverse colonial native tribes were counting on M. Papeleu and Denizart to defend their cause. Several other chiefs of the principal tribal peoples whom the mission would encounter throughout its planned itinerary would be speaking to the deputies in very similar terms on this topic. And, not alone would these chiefs and their tribes peoples claim voting rights, but also, the rights to be deemed eligible to stand as candidates for election to the French Parliament.

It is worth mentioning here that, during these discussions, M. Papeleu and M. Denizart maintained themselves in an attitude of prudent reserve, while simultaneously assuring the Kazembé chief that the Commission's report would contain the tribes's electoral claims, which would then be laid before the Government and Houses of Parliament for discussion and debate.

At the same time, Razzi repeated the invitation which he had formulated, for when the expedition would be on their return journey, departing from Brazzaville. He absolutely was counting on the eventuality that M. Deltour and his companions would return to

From *Adventures of Three Russians and Three Englishmen in Southern Africa.*

Loango by following along the south of the Congolese border and that they would enter into talks with the diverse tribes, including that of the Bassoundi, his own tribe, which would provide them with the warmest possible reception and welcome.

Upon the request of MM. Papeleu and Denizart, Nicolas Vanof assured the Kazembé people that such was indeed their intention, in order that the mission with which they were entrusted might achieve completion of all its necessary remits, to the satisfaction of all stakeholders concerned with the success of this fact-finding diplomatic visit.

From *The Astonishing Adventure of the Barsac Mission*.

And, in fact, this was how the plan of this fact-finding, exploratory mission was drawn up. It was necessary to benefit properly from previous explorations of this nature, of which Louis Merly, with the approval of M. André Deltour, had meticulously drawn up the full itinerary.

Having left Libreville, the caravan would thus head off in a straight line, by means of a series of stages conducted on foot, comprising two hundred and ten kilometres, in a south-easterly direction. The caravan would thus reach the right bank of the Ogooué which would be crossed by M. Deltour and his companions, together with the staff and material of the expedition.

Once this part of the passage had been effected, the caravan would resume its march across the plains and the bush country in such a way as to reach Lastourville, where it would remain for a stop-over sojourn of several days.

It was estimated that this first part of the journey—provided that unforeseen circumstances did not slow its onward progress—could be completed within less than four weeks.

In leaving Lastourville, or rather Madiville, the current name of this inland city, M. André Deltour, in the face of the impossibility of using the rivers of the region which are, for the most part, non-navigable, across the region of the Adoumas, would travel towards the right, towards Franceville, where he would stop, after a journey of two hundred kilometres.

There, in fact, would take place the second halt within one week, justified equally by the exhaustions of the journey and by the research needs of the fact-finding mission in this quite large colonial centre. Moreover, it would be advisable to stock up on fresh provisions in anticipation of the third stage of the exploratory journey, which was due to reach its goal at the right-hand bank of the great Congolese river.

Beyond this destination, it would be necessary to make preparations in order to allow for hard, demanding stages across a very savage territory, crossed by watercourses and crowned in parts with forests, and through which marching progress would be difficult. But, at one hundred and fifty kilometres from there, the caravan would then cross the Alima basin, a tributary of the Congo, and the canoes would have to do nothing more than safely abandon themselves to the flowing current of the river.

Once the confluence of rivers had been arrived at, transport would be by water for all of the personnel of the expedition, both by the steamships and by the canoes assigned to sailing upon the river, and this third stage of the journey, following a trek of eight hundred and fifty kilometres, would come to an end at Brazzaville.

At that location would take place the final major stopover of the Deltour mission, during which the investigation would be completed, on the question of the electorate and the voting eligibility of the resident colonists; as well as the question concerning the industrial and business development of the French Congo.

In accordance with the calculations made—which were, moreover, subject to possible revision—it would be towards the end of November that the expedition would reach Brazzaville, from whence would begin the fourth stage of the journey, which would set off in the direction of Loango, towards the coast, without neglecting, of course, to make the promised visits to Chief Razzi and to the other tribes who have set up encampments across the length of the southern border.

In such conditions, this fact-finding mission should, at its end, have lasted about three and a half months, provided that no incident or obstacle hindered its onward progress and march. As for the crossing from Loango to Libreville, that would take place aboard the packetboat which serves the main maritime points of the African coast along the Atlantic seaboard.

Such was the nature of the final, well-thought-out, well-prepared itinerary of travel and meetings, which had been maturely brought to fruition and which would allow, from all points of view, the accomplishment of the tasks with which our fact-finding explorers had been entrusted.

On the 9th September, after spending a week at Libreville, the mission was ready to set out on its journey, and the departure was definitively arranged to take place the following day. The material to be transported was all in a fit state, the parcels had been distributed amongst the porters for whom it now remained only to take their allotted charge upon their head and to follow, in lines of porters, the "capites" or local foremen or "roundhead" supervisors to whom they directly reported; as for the Senegalese marksmen, led by Sergeants Trost and Césaire, they would take up their positions as those persons of the rank of escort, some in front in order to scout out and reconnoitre the route, the others bringing up the rear in order to close ranks.

M. André Deltour, as well as his fellow mission-members, were really feeling itchy feet at this stage to begin their mission and get down to work, and with what feverish impatience had they not anticipated this finally arrived day of departure. And as for M. Isidore Papeleu and M. Joseph Denizart, they most assuredly shared this impatience to get going. For several weeks the two colleagues had, in their imagination, journeyed so extensively, that they were now burning with desire to finally find themselves travelling within complete, unadulterated reality.

All of the expedition personnel presented for duty in excellent form; as has been noted earlier, both the porters and the soldiers were likely to withstand, with great resistance, the exhaustions of the journey.

That evening, a final meeting was held at the Governor's Residence. The Governor had invited the city's civic and military authorities and dignitaries, and the final official farewells were to be delivered at the

From *The Astonishing Adventure of the Barsac Mission.*

end of this reception, which would be concluded with official glasses of punch, in the midst of cheers of "hurrah!"

The evening flowed on merrily. M. André Deltour, M. Louis Merly and Nicolas Vanof received good-natured congratulations and sincere best wishes for the success of the mission from all those in attendance, good wishes which, moreover, were not found wanting in being equally addressed to both the deputy of the Haute-Vienne and of the Lower Seine, who were strongly moved by these numerous wishes of *bon voyage*. Finally, the crowning point of the ceremony was a toast proposed by the Governor, M. H. Regnault, which was joined in by the exclamations of joy of all of the guests. And the official words of response delivered by M. André Deltour on behalf of his fellow expedition members and travelling companions was greeted with unanimous applause.

The evening came to a close at almost two o'clock in the morning, and, the next day, in the presence of the entire population, both

European and indigenous, the caravan left Libreville; and even when it had finally disappeared behind the last remaining houses, the cheers continued to reverberate.

Chapter V

STAGES OF THE JOURNEY

The early stages of the march of the expedition were to take place in favourable climatic conditions, even though the temperature was still hot, even in this month of September in a region of Equatorial latitude. Groups of clouds, pushed lightly through the skies by a medium breeze blowing from the open sea, softened the otherwise fiery heat of the sun. Furthermore, having left Libreville, there was no shortage of shelter, for the caravan, from the large overhanging trees, as the convoy wound its way downwards in a south-easterly direction in order to reach the left bank of the Ogooué.

Alongside the guide, Sergeant Trost marched at the head of one half of the escort of Senegalese marksmen. Following them next in the procession of the marching convoy were the various groups comprising the different members of the mission. M. Deltour and his travelling companions were dressed in clothes of light, soft flannel material, their head protected by the white canvas helmet with a protective piece of tissue of the size of a handkerchief attached to the helmet, in order to protect the nape of the neck from sunburn. Each of them wore his rifle in a bandoleer slung across the shoulder, and this included even the two Parliamentary colleagues who would not be the last to make use of this weapon if some attractive piece of game should happen to pass by within easy firing range. After all, didn't M. Isidore Papeleu and M. Joseph Denizart normally take part in the Presidentially-organized hunts in Marly and Compiègne?

At a short distance behind came the porters, with their load carried upon their head, with chest and arms bare, their feet hardened by the

From *The Astonishing Adventure of the Barsac Mission.*

From *A Fifteen-Year-Old Captain.*

long march, following in a two-by-two line, in accordance with the orders of their foremen.

Then, the other half of the escort of Senegalese marksmen made up the last ranks of the procession, bringing up the rear, under the orders of Sergeant Césaire.

The stages of this first day of travel were undertaken along the right bank of that estuary of which Libreville occupies a point, close to the coast. The marchers walked on a ground upon which clay was mixed with sand. It was a roasting-hot surface, sun-scorched and sun-baked, so to speak, by the fierce, burning rays of the sun over this Equatorial region.

ILLUSTRATIONS

One of the challenges in the Palik series is selecting illustrations, derived from the first French publication of Verne stories in the 19th century and the beginning of the 20th century. Most are either from the stories with which they appeared, or are from other Verne stories, choosing images to match the new context. In this volume, the engravings from *The Somber Fate of Jean Morénas* are from the original French publication in *Hier et Demain*, while those for *Pierre-Jean* and *Fact-Finding Mission* are from other Verne stories. Only those depicting actual historical persons or events are from other sources.

We are particularly indebted to **Bernhard Krauth**, chairman of the German Jules-Verne-Club since 2005, for providing the illustrations from Verne stories. A deep sea licensed master working today as a docking pilot in Bremerhaven, Germany, Bernhard has published several Verne-related articles in France, the Netherlands and Germany. Intensely interested in the illustrations of the original French editions of Verne's work, he has been deeply involved in a project to digitize the illustrations, more than 5,000 in all. The project is for common, non-commercial use, and most of the illustrations in this publication were made possible through his generosity.

Acknowledgements

The Palik series, while spearheaded by the North American Jules Verne Society, represents a cooperative effort among Vernians worldwide, pooling the resources and knowledge of the various organizations in different countries. The Society is grateful for research assistance to Frédéric Jaccaud, curator of Jean-Michel Margot's Verne Collection at the Maison d'Ailleurs (House of Elsewhere) in Yverdon-les-Bains, Switzerland. The City of Nantes (Frances), whose Municipal Library has placed all Jules Vernes manuscripts online, helped make this publication possible, and the Society would like to thank the City of Nantes and its Bibliothèque municipale (director: Agnès Marcetteau) for their ongoing assistance.

The Society also appreciates the efforts of members who have contributed to this volume, including Malcolm Henderson and Ross Bagby, as well as such friends as Jean Frodsham, Elvira Berkowitsch, and Pachara Yongvongpaibul.

CONTRIBUTORS

KIERAN O'DRISCOLL has recently been awarded his Ph.D. in Verne literary translation, by Dublin City University. His doctoral thesis was entitled *Around the World in Eighty Changes: A diachronic study of six complete translations (1873-2004), from French to English, of Jules Verne's novel, Le Tour du Monde en Quatre-Vingts Jours (1873)*, and explored the multiple causes of Verne retranslations. The monograph version was titled *Retranslation Through The Centuries: Jules Verne in English*, published in 2011 by Peter Lang Ltd. Kieran holds a B.A. in Applied Languages (French and Spanish) with International Marketing Communications (2003) from Waterford Institute of Technology, and an M.A. in Translation Studies (2005) from Dublin City University, both degrees with First Class Honours. His Master's dissertation focused on the translations into French of J.K. Rowling's Harry Potter series. He has lectured in French at third-level, and in Advanced English as a Foreign Language, and has also done professional literary translation. Before entering academia, Kieran worked for almost twenty years in Irish local government, and also holds academic qualifications in Public Administration, Law and Music (Pianoforte).

BRIAN TAVES (Ph.D., University of Southern California) has been an archivist in the Motion Picture, Broadcasting, and Recorded Sound Division of the Library of Congress since 1990. He is the author of over 100 articles and 25 chapters in anthologies. Taves has also written books on P.G. Wodehouse and Hollywood; director Robert Florey; the genre of historical adventure movies; and fantasy-adventure writer Talbot Mundy, in addition to editing an original anthology of Mundy's best stories. In 2002-2003, Taves was chosen as Kluge Staff Fellow at the Library to write the first book on silent film pioneer Thomas Ince, to appear in 2011. Taves's writing on Verne has been translated into French, German, and Spanish, and he is currently writing a book on the 300 film and television adaptations of Verne worldwide. Taves is coauthor of *The Jules Verne Encyclopedia* (Scarecrow, 1996), and edited the first English-language publication of Verne's *Adventures of the Rat Family* (Oxford, 1993).

THE PALIK SERIES

The last two decades have brought astonishing progress in the study of Jules Verne, with new translations of Verne stories, including the discovery of many texts. Still, there remain a number of Verne stories that have been overlooked, and it is this gap that the North American Jules Verne Society seeks to fill in the Palik series.

The North American Jules Verne Society (NAJVS) was formed in 1993, and a decade later, underwrote *Journey Through the Impossible*, the first complete edition in any language of Verne's 1882 science fiction theatrical spectacle, *Voyage à travers l'impossible*. With this experience, and thanks to the generosity of the Society's late member, Edward Palik, a series was commenced to bring to the Anglophone public a series of hitherto unknown Verne tales.

Ed Palik had a special enthusiasm for bringing neglected Verne stories to English-speaking readers, and this will be reflected in the series that bears his name. In this way the Society hopes to fulfill the goal that Ed's consideration has made possible, along with the assistance of a variety of Verne translators and scholars from around the world. The volumes in the Palik series will reveal the amazing range of Verne's storytelling, in genres that may surprise those who only know his most famous stories. We hope to allow a better appreciation of the famous writer who has, for more than a century and a half, been the widest-read author of fiction in the world.

PREVIOUS VOLUMES

The Marriage of a Marquis

Jules Verne is the acclaimed author of such pioneering science fiction as *20,000 Leagues Under the Sea* and *Journey to the Center of the Earth*. Yet he also wrote much more, including stories never before translated into English, which will be presented for the first time in the Palik series, under the auspices of the North American Jules Verne Society.

Foreshadowing such classics as *Around the World in 80 Days*, this inaugural volume focuses on two of Verne's earliest humorous stories, *The Marriage of Mr. Anselme des Tilleuls* and *Jédédias Jamet, or The Tale of an Inheritance*. Translation is provided by Edward Baxter and Kieran O'Driscoll, two of the leading Verne experts; critical commentary examines both stories, and scholars explore why some of the author's stories were overlooked for so many years.

Shipwrecked Family: Marooned with Uncle Robinson

Castaway by pirates on a deserted island… without tools or supplies to survive… a mother and her children have only a kindly old sailor to help. But what explains the strange flora and fauna they find?

The second volume in the Palik series, presented by the North American Jules Verne Society, offers another story never before published in English. *Shipwrecked Family* was rejected by Verne's publisher, so rather than finish it, he began to rewrite it with new characters—and that became the classic, *The Mysterious Island*, where Captain Nemo made his last appearance. Here, then, is Verne's first draft of that novel, one which is very different from the book that it became.

Translation is provided by Sidney Kravitz, also translator of the definitive modern edition of *The Mysterious Island*.

Mr. Chimp and Other Plays

Long before Verne stories had formed the basis for such movies as *Around the World in 80 Days*, many of his plays were theatrical blockbusters on the 19th century stage, including several from his novels. In this volume, expert scholarly research introduces four of Verne's plays written in his youth, translated by Frank Morlock. Included are *The Knights of the Daffodil*, *Mr. Chimpanzee*, *An Adoptive Son*, and *Eleven Day of Siege*. Verne's themes range from romantic comedies to a scientist's discovery that there may not be such a difference between human and ape after all!

Even as he became a novelist, the stage remained crucial to Verne. In 2002, the North American Jules Verne Society published (through Prometheus) the first English translation of Verne's science fiction play, *Journey Through the Impossible*. Of that volume, the Washington Science Fiction Association commented, "A work for Verne aficionados, theater buffs, or just those who enjoy a good story…. See another side of the 'Father of Science Fiction.'"

The Count of Chanteleine: A Tale of the French Revolution

This adventure is for everyone who has thrilled to *The Scarlet Pimpernel*, *A Tale of Two Cities*, or *Scaramouche*. A nobleman, the Count of Chanteleine, leads a rebellion against the revolutionary French government. While he fights for the monarchy and the church, his home is destroyed and his wife murdered by the mob. Now he must save his daughter from the guillotine. This exciting swashbuckler is also a meticulous historical re-creation of a particularly bloody episode in the Reign of Terror.

The Count of Chanteleine is the first English translation of this Jules Verne novel, the fourth volume in the Palik series published under the auspices of the North American Jules Verne Society. Commentary by an international team of experts supports the translation by Edward Baxter.

Additional volumes are underway.

www.ingramcontent.com/pod-product-compliance
Lightning Source LLC
Chambersburg PA
CBHW072354030726
47505CB00014B/1824